THE DYING SWAN

Lindsay Marie Docherty

ISBN: 9798336006551

Words Lindsay Marie Docherty ©2024

Additional front cover artwork - Meek ©2024

Original image "In Your Dying Arms I Lay" ©2024

Lindsay has asserted her moral rights

First edition published by

Inherit The Earth

In conjunction with Amazon

All Rights Reserved

2024

This book is dedicated to the memory of beloved sister Kirsty Louise Carol McKenna

Lindsay
August
2024

Spread Your Wings

It was so, so dark and cold, she could feel the freezing concrete on her skin, and she was hungry. The bounds to her ankles and wrist cut into her flesh which made the tiniest movement painful. She was trying not to cry, and then she heard his footsteps. She wouldn't let herself scream, couldn't let him see her absolute fear. She went to a place in her mind that she could escape. She thought of things she wanted to do in life, achievements yet to be accomplished. She wanted to stroke and comfort elephants in a rescue sanctuary, sit with wolves and observe them, kiss a boy, go to university, swim in the wild sea. She felt him touch her face; she bit him like a rabid dog.

Tess woke with a jump, fear shot through her. She reached to the side of the bed and grabbed the paper bag and began to breathe slowly and deeply into it until the anxiety washed away like a sandcastle as the sea came in. She clambered out of bed, took a quick shower and got dressed. Her long blond hair lay wet around her shoulders. "Shit," she had packed the hair dryer and was damned if she could remember in which box. She wrapped a towel around her head and proceeded into the kitchen to make tea and toast. There was no time for a run this morning, plus she was sick of breathing in the polluted thick London air that descended on them more in this summer heat. She had packed all her favourite and essential possessions, the rest she had left for charity. Tess wanted a clean break, a fresh start. She had money left over from the sale of her London flat and managed to buy a lovely apartment in the West End of Glasgow. New country, new beginnings. She had never actually been to view her new place; it had all been done online. However, as her dad was Glaswegian, she knew the area well and also Glasgow by heart. Tess loaded her car up with boxes ignoring the double yellow lines. Locked up the flat, posted her spare keys through the letterbox as the estate agent had another set for the new owners and off, she went. The drive would be a long one.

She had floored the car, breaking speed limits and she chuckled to herself over that and her parking all in one day. Tess, perfect Tess who always acknowledged the law had a newfound rebellion. She waited until she had crossed the border then pulled into a service station. She ordered a Vegan sausage roll and black tea, found a place to sit then pulled out her mobile.

"Hi, could I speak to Doctor Maclean please? It's Tess O'Brien." She was put on hold a moment then Dr Maclean's velvety voice answered.

"Hi Tess, hope the journey is, OK? Shall we give you a few days to settle in then start work say Wednesday?"

"That would be perfect, looking forward to it"

"Brilliant, so pleased to have you on board Tess, See you then,"

"Goodbye Dr Maclean."

"Bye Tess."

She wolfed down her food and drink, headed to the ladies, and once back in her car put her foot down again. She rolled down her window breathing in this glorious clean air, turned on the radio and headed for Glasgow.

She arrived in the West End and went straight to the estate agents to pick up her keys and parking permit. She glanced in the window to see luxurious houses and flats for sale, this area had it all, pubs, clubs, museums, galleries, hip little eateries and expensive restaurants. She entered the building, the insides were plush and comfortable, not office like at all. The estate agent who served her gave her the creeps; he kept running his eyes all over her body.

"Could I just take your ID, Mrs, or is it, Miss?"

"Actually, it's Doctor, Doctor O'Brien."

"Oh, brains as well?" He leeched as he checked her passport and driving license. "Ok, here you go, if there is anything at all, just phone me."

"Sure, thanks," she made a face as she left the shop.

She was really tired from the drive, but she pulled up into her parking space and smiled. The tenement was stunning, a grand imposing building.

She could hardly contain her excitement as she leaped from the car like a kid going to the beach. She took the stairs two at a time; her flat was on the top floor. She looked for number 10b, found it put the key in her door and entered the flat. It took her breath away, the beautiful parquet flooring was so shiny, the entrance grand with exquisite coving and panels that had been painted with expensive sage green paint. The entrance gave way to a large sitting room with French doors leading to a wrought iron balcony. She opened the doors and inhaled deeply. Although she had seen the flat online, nothing prepared her for the magnificent views over Kelvingrove Park. Her tiredness suddenly evaporated, which was a good job as she had no furniture as she wanted to get a feel for the flat first. Tess took her boxes up to the flat and then decided to check out the gorgeous little second hand and antique shops that littered the area. She came across the perfect shop, near Partick. She chose an antique French slay bed, antique wardrobes and drawers and two mismatching sofas, after all they went with her eclectic taste. The owner promised delivery that evening, and Tess informed him she was on the third floor. That would be a great workout for two poor souls. She thanked the owner and left. Then headed for the supermarket; ah, the brilliance of supermarkets where you can buy food and all your white goods at the same time. Delivery of those would be tomorrow so she would eat out tonight. She texted her old uni friend to see if she would like to join her, it was a girl date, 7pm tonight at a cosy local pub that was renowned for its good food. She showered again, found which box her hairdryer was in, dried her hair and pulled on grey skinny jeans, a casual blouse knee high boots and a faux leather jacket. She looked in her mirror, which was still leaning against the wall, she was 5 foot 7 and willowy, stunning that's what people called her, both men and women, but she sometimes felt it was a curse.

There was a knock on her door and for a moment she was a little puzzled before realising it would be the delivery men. The man at the door breathed heavily after taking the stairs with her deliveries, she opened the door, and they moved in the furniture. Tess asked them to put it all in the living room otherwise she would be late. She tipped the men 20 pounds each and thanked them as they left.

Tess entered the pub and immediately loved the vibrant atmosphere, the music not too loud and not too quiet, traditional music. She headed for the bar knowing that with her tiredness the drink would go straight to her head. She ordered one bottle of white wine and two snakebites for old times' sake. The bartender told her to take a seat and he would bring the drinks over, with a cheeky wink. She winked back and flashed a smile that could break a million hearts. Just as she took her seat someone tapped her on the shoulder. "Well, well, well, our beautiful Tess is now a Glaswegian."

Tess turned to see her friend's old familiar face, stood up and embraced her tightly.

"Oh, Jinty, I have missed you so much."

"Ok, let me go, you and your bloody hugs." Jinty and Tess both sat back down and laughed at the snake bite.

"I hope you don't mind I have ordered food."

"Oh wonderful, vegan no doubt, with this body do I look like a vegan?"

"There is nothing wrong with your body, it's your mind that's fucked up," Tess grinned as the waiter brought over two vegan curries.

"So, tell me all about your new flat, your new job and how stupid Sean ever let you go?" Jinty grinned as she said this, Tess new she had always hated Sean.

Tess tried not to choke on her snake bite.

"Well, the flat is stunning, the job I just can't believe I got it, and stupid Sean is still stupid but no longer my problem," she grinned.

"You can't believe you got the job, are you kidding? A first in archaeology under graduate, a distinction in your Masters, then a PHD in Osteoarchaeology and burial, girl stop being so modest."

Jinty took a huge swig of her snakebite, and then wiped her mouth with her sleeve. Tess adored her, she never changed she was just like she was in her student days; funny, feisty and blunt. People would never put these two together as friends, Jinty was short and rotund, cruel people called her plain. Tess, however, just saw a beautiful person who had held her hands through all her nightmares and anxiety attacks. She even missed classes to look after Tess when she really needed it. Apart from her very close relatives, police and courts, Jinty was the only person she had ever confided in about what happened to her as a teenager. In honour of that close bond Jinty had asked Tess to be godmother to both her young children, Tess had eagerly accepted, though she hoped nothing ever happened to Jinty as the kids were wild. The Bhuna tasted delicious, cauliflower, onions and tomatoes had been cooked in a rich, smooth and spicy sauce. They scooped up the curry with chapatis in traditional style. For a non-vegan Jinty soon polished off her curry, as did Tess, both of them famished.

"How are the kids, I will be able to see them so much more now?"

"Fucking hard work, I've had nae sleep in three years. Job, tell me about your job?"

Tess poured two glasses of wine and took a sip first.

"So, I was at the end of my PHD when I received an email from a Doctor Maclean up hear in Glasgow. He said he had been following my research carefully and wanted me on his team. He flew down to London interviewed me and offered me the job there and then."

She took another sip of wine.

"So what's your role? Is it laboratory, field or both?" Jinty started rolling a fag.

"You still smoking? God, Jinty." Tess picked up the roll up and inhaled the tobacco.

"Fuck off Tess, you hate me smoking but love the smell" Jinty grinned.

"So it's complicated, a little of my time will be lecturing students, and research, but the actual role is linked to police forensic investigations, United nations, and other organisations all over the world, exhumation of skeletons, investigating large burial sites found in places like the former Yugoslavia, or murder sites, it will be so interesting Jinty."

"Oh, how cool, and here's me the teacher, with my potty mouth."

Jinty and Tess both laughed at that. I mean of all jobs, Jinty a teacher.

"And you are definitely rid of Sean?"

Tess sighed, "Well fair to say it ended when I found him in bed with his student." They laughed again; Jinty has this brilliant gift of turning any shitty situation into a comedy. This is the remedy Tess needed.

"Fuck him, or not in this case, there are plenty of hot Scottish men who I am sure would love to date you."

"Do not set me up! Remember that stoner in uni you set me up with, just sat stoned picking his nose and eating it, yuck," Jinty chuckled.

"Aye, but he was English," They laughed and laughed.

They finished up their wine and decided to leave as it was a school night, especially for Jinty. Jinty sparked up her fag as soon as they got outside.

"Right, taxi home or I'm walking you," Jinty commanded.

"It's a few streets away, plus I have moved from London you know."

Jinty flagged down a taxi.

"I know you have but I also know you Tess, I know you still have nightmares and panic attacks, so no arguing. I'll drop you off first then I will head home."

Tess knew better than to argue with her old friend, you would never win. With that they both jumped in the taxi.

Drip, drip, drip. Oh that noise was like torture, she tried to curl in a ball as near to the wall as she could as he approached. His flashlight was suddenly upon her, hurting her eyes, she blinked rapidly trying to adjust.

"I've brought you food and water, eat and drink, hurry up." He was crouched in front of her his voice menacing.

"I, I, can't eat with these on my hands," she held out her shaking hands towards him, in a pleading gesture.

"Ha, do you think I'm stupid? The last time you nearly bit my fucking cheek off! I'll be scarred for life you little bitch."

She looked up at him and smirked, it took all her bravery but she was pleased his face was a mess. Why was this happening to her? Oh God, she just wanted her mum and dad, but she needed to keep brave, she sensed he took pleasure in her distress.

Her captor tore the sandwich into bits and forcefully fed her, she was nearly choking. He wouldn't let her finish chewing and swallowing before he forced more into her mouth. She gulped as fast as she could, he then forced the water bottle into her mouth and she drank greedily. She caught sight of his face; she had ripped his cheek wide open, looked like he had stitched it himself. She found comfort in his pain. She went to her safe place in her head, elephants, wolves, and the beach.

Tess, woke mid scream, told herself to calm down, she took slow deep breaths.

She could hear a dripping noise; she looked around her to see she had camped out in her living room. She walked towards the noise, shaking as she did so. It was the kitchen tap, she tried in vain to get it to stop dripping but to no avail, a tear fell down her cheek and she wiped it away.

She found her mobile and texted Jinty ;
Jinty, could you find me a plumber, it's the tap, its dripping, I can't listen to it ☹

Jinty texted back straight away;
On it. My brother-in-law is a plumber. I will have him come round about 5? Will you be ok? I can skip school?

Jinty, I can't let you do that, the plumber will do just fine! Love you xxx

Jinty texted back! *Ditto love xxx*

Tess needed therapy and Tess's therapy was running. She looked through her boxes and found her running gear, threw it on, jumped in the car and headed for Loch Lomond. She parked up, the car park was crammed full of tourists and there were coaches everywhere. She put in her earphones, found her running tunes, picked up her bottle of water and off she went.

The pure air in her lungs felt amazing, she needed to push herself hard, she headed for a track that circled part of the Loch, and she ran so fast to get away from those nightmares. She had pushed herself so hard for a few miles, she bent down and took a breather, then stood up. The view took her breath away; the Loch was stunning, surrounded by majestic Munros that challenged her to climb them, to see the delights that would await her once she reached their peak. The Loch was busy, boat trips, people taking a dip, people on the track walking their dogs, kids learning how to ride their shiny bikes. This is how life was supposed to be. At that moment she knew she had made the right decision, that her life would change forever. She looked up to the sky, felt the glorious sun on her face and off she darted again, the endorphins releasing in her brain, a natural beautiful chemical high.

Tess thanked the plumber as he left, then picked up her phone to call Jinty.

"Hey Jints, it's me Tess, just wondering if you wanted to come round and see the flat, have a few glasses of wine tonight?" Tess kicked off her running shoes and massaged her feet.

"Oh, kids have some vomiting bug and the shits, total chaos."

"Ok another time."

"Of course I'll come over, did you not hear me, I don't do shit and vomit."

Tess laughed as she heard Jinty shouting at her poor husband in the background.

"Sorted, they're his kids as well, are you cooking?" Jinty sniggered.

"Hey, do not laugh at my cooking it's better these days, see you soon you complete cow!" She hung up and chuckled to herself.

Tess took a shower and let the waves of water engulf her. She put on her comfy jogging suit and slippers. She went into the kitchen and started preparing the food, salad, vegan chilli with rice and bread sounded good. She started preparing the food, the spices hitting her nostrils as she did.

Jinty, never one for knocking sauntered in.

"Wow, nice place," she said as she walked in every room to look.

"It's fabulous and in such a good spot. It's a nice evening so thought we could sit on the balcony and eat?"

Jinty followed Tess to the balcony, where a large bottle of white wine sat in a cooler full of ice, two large glasses sat on the shabby chic table. Tess had bought an arrangement of potted plants that were dotted round the balcony. Jinty knew that Tess wouldn't just place these anywhere, she will have re-arranged them multiple times and looked at them from all angles before she was satisfied they were in the right spot. Jinty could smell the aroma of spices and garlic, her stomach grumbled.

They both sat and Tess poured the wine.

"Tess, could you do me a favour and start locking your door, it unnerves me," she looked at Tess concerned.

"Oh, yes mum, of course mum," she picked up her wine and took a sip.

"Thank you and less of your sarcasm. So have you heard from Sean the shit?"

"Nope, I'm hoping it stays that way. I have nothing left to say to him. You know Jinty in the five years we were together not once did he bother to ask about my nightmares, he didn't really know me at all."

"Well that says it all, plus he doesn't deserve to know you. Let's raise our glasses to life without Sean the shit." They both raised their glasses and clinked them together. Then burst out laughing like schoolgirls.

"So you left poor Mark with kids with the shits?"

"Yup, he cancelled his lads' night" she winked

"You have a damn good one there Jinty, don't forget that."

"He knew what I was like when he married me, stubborn, opinionated and crass." She poured more wine for them both.

"You forgot, loyal, loving, caring, and funny as fuck, to name but a few." It was Tess's turn to wink.

She brought out the food which was steaming hot and they sat contented while they ate and people-watched from her balcony. The evening was buzzing with people, students mulled about, people came home from work, and others went into the park to enjoy the evening sun. They sat there for hours, reminiscing about their university days, their lives, Jinty's family and Tess's job. It was getting late so off Jinty went home to the madness of poorly children. Tess put the dishes in the dishwasher, changed into her nightwear and went to bed; her gigantic antique French bed awaited her like something from a fairy-tale. She would get a happy ending too.

Drip, drip drip, that noise, God that noise. Her captor had improved her conditions a little, she had a mattress and only her hands remained shackled, he had left a thick duvet to protect her from the cold, he had provide water within reach and bread. Her ears pricked, she thought she heard scratching and whining. Oh, was there another girl somewhere near? Someone like her. She bit her lip as she thought of her parents, how worried they would be. She thought of Jude her beautiful Jude. She pulled the duvet up to her chin. She would have to try sleep, what use would she be if she had no strength?

Tess woke with a start, but a start was better than screaming, or feeling like she couldn't breathe. She threw off the duvet; she would start her day with a run round Kelvingrove Park, then head to work for the first time.

The Archaeologist

Tess parked up and headed into the University of Glasgow, her new work place. She had to pinch herself, it didn't feel real. She wore a very low heel and was casual smart, realistically she was more comfortable in the archaeologists' gear of knee pads, waterproofs, dirty clothes and her special little trowel. People were often shocked when she informed them of her vocation, if she asked them to guess most would say model or beautician something that was stereotypical of a stunning woman. This annoyed Tess as people presumed you couldn't have both beauty and brains, they just didn't get that she was in her element deep in dirt, mud, and God knows what.

Tess walked towards the academics offices, one of which now had a notice with her name on. She could not suppress a smile. Dr Maclean was waiting in Tess's office admiring the view of trees and shrubs. When she entered he turned round with a beaming smile and outstretched his hand. She took his hand, shook it, and smiled back.

"Welcome on board Tess, this is all so exciting. Can I get you a tea or coffee?"

"Oh, a Tea black would be great thanks."

He walked towards the door to go get their drinks. Tess liked his humility, he was so well renowned in the archaeological community for his research, dedication and writing but he was humble, she admired that quality. He came back through the door with two large mugs in his hands, and gestured for her to take the main seat at her desk. She pulled an excited face as she did.

"So now we have you here, if I could just go over our schedule, etc as there is some teaching and supervising involved getting students through their dissertations. Though the main point of both our roles is to be on hand for the police not only here but also abroad. So it's an international position too and the first roles of their kind. With that in mind I have your teaching and supervising down to just 2 days per week, as we also need to concentrate on our research together. So it's a mixture really and an exciting one at that."

"I just can't wait to get started and to pick your brains, it's all so exciting and I am privileged you appointed me."

"Well that was the easy part; I had, as you know, become aware of your own research and work, so for me too it is a privilege. You will excel in this role, but not only that it will stimulate your brain. With that I will leave you to walk round the campus and familiarise yourself again as I am sure things have changed since your undergraduate days. There are the keys to your office and a locker. I have supervision to do so I must run but I will catch you later. Bye Tess, or Doctor if you prefer."

"Tess is just fine, and you?"

"Oh just David will do," with that he grabbed his coat and was off.

The first place Tess headed for was the Osteo lab, as any Osteoarchaeologists would. She climbed a flight of stairs with a spring and jump in her step. The lab was at the end of a long narrow corridor. She opened the doors and entered her playground. Row after row of remains both human and animal were on show. Fake full-life skeletons were also dotted around for educational purposes. For some this would be their worst nightmare or a scene from a Halloween film, but for Tess it gets her adrenalin running and her blood pumping. Her brain springs into action accessing the many skulls for sign of injury and trauma. She can see the sword mark on one of the skulls, a fatal blow through the top of the skull. She can look at the state of the teeth for evidence of diet and through analysis even determines where that person grew up. She drew a deep breath and savoured this moment, she took out her schedule and noted she would be teaching tomorrow morning, then contacting some Master's students about their dissertation topics and emailing them her research topics.

She left the lab and familiarised herself with the campus. She located the toilets, café, and library first, although all journals could now be found on the university search or through google scholar. She simply loved the quietness and the smell of books, there was something so comforting in that. Her fondness took her back to her dark past. She had to grow up too fast and her early teenage years stolen from her along with her dignity and worse. She didn't have the carefree attitude of most teenagers, going out to discos getting drunk, enjoying their first kiss. So she ploughed herself into studying, sought solace in the library. Some thought she was very macabre as she was so obsessed with death and burial, then later Osteoarchaeology. She was, but the subjects were often dark, skeletons had faced trauma, disease, injury, she could resonate and empathise with them, they felt the feelings she had felt, the fear excruciating fear, confusion, and despair. Most living people hadn't experienced that. Sometimes she had better relationships with the dead than the living. She stopped herself from thinking about those days, she put her work cap back on and left to grab some dinner. She felt like the new kid at school. She grabbed an expresso and ordered a vegan sausage sandwich, she wanted comfort food. She found a table sat down and enjoyed her lunch as she read a journal article. As she did a man approached her table.

"Excuse me are you Dr O'Brien," he asked

"Hi, yes that's me. Can I help you?"

"Yes, sorry for the intrusion, I thought I would introduce myself, I'm Jack McStay I'm head of excavation, it's very thrilling to have you here."

"Oh, thank you I'm pleased to meet you, I have to run now but maybe we could catch lunch during the week, I'd love to hear about your digs?"

"That would be great I'll drop you an email to see when suits, catch you during the week, see you later."

"Brilliant, goodbye" she said and with that he strode off towards the exit, he looked every inch head of excavation, muddy boots, tools, and archaeologist's hat. He looked to be about 60, a grey ponytail hung from the bottom of his neck. She would enjoy talking to him, he looked like a character.

She headed back to her office to fire off some emails and check her won. Jack McStay had emailed to say he would be free Friday if she was. She replied to say she would be too and arranged their lunch. She checked her watch and was surprised to see it was home time, she grabbed her bag, coat and laptop and headed for her car.
Once home she took a long soak in her roll top bath, candles lit so she could relax. She put on her pyjamas, a little early but she wasn't going out again and just wanted to chill. Her phone rang an unknown number flashed on screen.

"Hi, it's Tess O'Brien, Doctor O'Brien, how can I help?"

"It's me, Sean, don't hang up Tess please just hear me out?"

"Are you fucking for real, I've moved on Sean what do you want?" She was so angry, she hadn't smoked since uni, but Jinty had left a packet of cigs by mistake, Tess grabbed one, opened the balcony door, lit it and inhaled.

"Tess, I made a huge mistake, I'll do anything to get you back, Tess," he whined down the phone, only now had it dawned on her that he had a whining voice, it irritated the shit out if her.

The nicotine hit her brain and she swayed as it made her feel dizzy.

"Now you listen to me Sean, do not ever call me again, this is a new chapter, my new chapter and you are history, now fuck off."

She ended the call, then stubbed out the cig angrily, I won't let that fucker make me smoke she thought.

The Artist And His Muse

He stood back and admired his work, well the first part at least, this would be brilliant but not his masterpiece, he was saving that for someone else. She laid on her back, long blond hair flaying around her shoulders, arms in a prayer pose, long legs stretched one foot resting on the other. The girl lay on a swan's wing, her head was slightly titled towards the west, and her face was a blur at this moment in time. It wouldn't remain that way, however, his muse for now was still alive, she wouldn't stay that way. He smirked at the thought, his art and her spirituality in death would be captured forever. She was beautiful; he hoped she appreciated why he had chosen her, though no one would ever match his first muse. He was angry for a moment when he thought of her, bitch; she hadn't appreciated his art, the context of it, the ancestry, the history, all his work she had tarnished.

This was the weirdest job the girl had ever done, but very well paid. She had answered an advertisement for a model? He had picked her up as agreed at Carlisle station, stupid she knew, but he was really pleasant. He was a bit reclusive, an artist. He was very posh too. She couldn't believe her luck when they crossed the border into Scotland and pulled up outside a huge castle. Although he was much older than her, 50's she daydreamed of being his wife and living here. Uni could wait she grinned to herself. Not bad for a girl out of the care system.

All he really wanted her to do was pose for his art, not really her thing but better than being asked to do porn. Plus she got to stay here and paid amazingly well, in cash. He fed her well, plus lots of champagne flowing which she could get used to. She was lying on the bed in a white gown he had asked her to wear, she did everything he asked. He had said something about a dying swan, he wanted to capture her beauty, her elegant neck long like a swans. She slowly moved back to the perfect position, his perfect position, the dead swan.

2011

Move like Jagger by Maroon 5 blasted from the radio. She looked at her reflection in the mirror. Anyone looking in would see the most beautiful 17 year old girl; all she could see was rot. Her parents had nipped out, very unlike them to leave her, however she had insisted they go for a meal. She had taken some of her parents wine from the rack in the kitchen. In her bedroom she necked it from the bottle, took the lid off the pills gulped down the lot then lay on her bed. She was drifting off or dying when she saw a picture of an elephant in her mind's eye, she reached out to touch its trunk. You've not even met an elephant yet, the trunk felt strange like a curly wire, she realised the trunk was the old phone wire she had in her room. She was grasping it. She was struggling to open her eyes, it felt like her soul was swimming through mud trying to reach the surface, everything was dark and foggy; she made it to the surface and opened her eyes. She needed to act quickly. She dialled 999.

2022 Glasgow

Tess was wakened at 5 AM by her mobile sounding.

"Oh, fuck off," she said as she fumbled by her bed for her phone.

"Sigh, yes?"

"Tess, sorry it's so early, it's David."

"David," her brain was scrambled.

"Dr Maclean, Tess we need to be ready in an hour and then head down to Cumbria. There's a skeleton, Tess. It's got our name on it, a local farmer unearthed it. I'll pick you up. 1 hour."
She waited outside her flat, she had jumped in the shower, grabbed a strong coffee, hair up, casuals on jeans and t-shirt. She had a bag packed for the excavation, also a bag of very smart clothes in case of a press conference or interview. She had little make-up but she didn't really need it.

David (Dr Maclean) pulled up in his Land Rover; it had seen better days like most archaeologists' vehicles. She jumped in and they headed for the M74, they chatted a while then she dozed off.

She woke with a start, self-consciously checked for drool. She pulled the mirror down as they made their way into Carlisle centre and checked her appearance, oh fuck she thought at her reflection, no wonder Sean shagged his student if she looked this bad when she woke up. David glanced in her direction.

"I think we need breakfast before we get to the police station for our briefing," he raised his eyebrows.

"Hell yes, I can't think straight without food." She brushed her hair into a neat ponytail; they parked up at a local café and went for breakfast.

A larger-than-life waitress approached them and dumped menus on their table. Shit, you wouldn't argue with her even if she got the order wrong. After a while she approached their table, David ordered full breakfast and Tess the vegan option. The waitress wore a name badge that screamed Vera.

"You can have full English or full Scottish, we do both."

Tess could not determine whether her accent was English or Scottish, it was like a mongrel accent.
"When in England," David replied, smiling a little mockingly.

Their order arrived, David's was a grand affair, all singing and dancing while Tess's was mushrooms, hash browns, beans, toast. It tasted so good, she washed it down with tea and lots of sugar. She needed the hit.

"Are you ready, Tess?" David's question had a question within a question. She nodded and off they went.

They parked up in Carlisle's main police quarters, the summer heat hit Tess as she got out of the air-conditioned car, wow, she never thought she would find northern summers so hot. The building was a 1970s square affair. Under threat of being demolished, like most 60's and 70's monstrosities. She had a friend, a former PHD student too, Sara, who had a passion for modern archaeology and saving it. Her argument was a good one; that we demolish everything from these eras as we see them as ugly, but if we carry on we will have nothing left. Her friend had campaigned for the iconic but ugly Bradford and Bingley building society building in Bingley West Yorkshire to be saved. It hadn't worked and the site was demolished much to her friend's anger. She would have to call Sara; she hadn't spoken to her in ages. David pushed open the door and in they went towards the reception desk. They explained who they were and were shown through to a large office. The office was full of men, she assumed these were the detectives who would be working the case. She and David sat on chairs that resembled those uncomfortable school chairs, like you couldn't possibly learn and be comfy at the same time. Most of the men stared at her, actually all of them did, she was used to it but it still annoyed her and she felt self-conscious. David asked her if she was OK, she nodded. People were chattering away but all went quiet as the door opened and a stocky man entered the room. Now it was her turn to stare, he was utterly beautiful. He obviously worked out his muscles were straining to get out of his suit. He was about 5 ft. 11 and had the most intense blue eyes she had ever seen. He spoke with a thick Glaswegian accent and scanned the room as he did. He introduced himself as Patrick, then bellowed

"Where the fuck is Martin?"

It felt like no one dare to answer him.

"Someone, anyone? For fuck sake he was out last night, do you think I'm stupid?"

He frowned as the room stayed silent.

"Right then, I believe you're both forensic archaeologists sent here to tell us how to do our job?" Collectively the room sniggered

Tess looked at David, he was absolutely furious, as was she.

"I'm Doctor Maclean and this is Dr O'Brien and you will all address us as such. We are here to help, not have a war or show you how to do your job." David stood up, "may we see you in your office?"

Patrick sarcastically did a bow and waved his hands towards the door, Tess felt eyes boring into her ass as she left the room. Jesus, she didn't know David had it in him to shout, but he sure did, he wasn't going to take Patrick's insults lying down.

"Detective Inspector, how dare you insult me and my good colleague? We are here because we specialise in forensic and Osteoarchaeology, nothing more, there maybe things your untrained eye would miss, we are not at bastard school, we're all grownups. Now we can either work together or we can go away back to Glasgow, leave you too it and miss critical evidence and/or interpretation. We are all here for the victim surely, not our egos?" he swallowed hard and shrugged his hands in his pockets. Tess thought that might've been to stop himself taking a swing for Patrick.

"You will both address me as Detective Inspector Donovan, don't get in my fucking way and don't give me this superior academic bullshit. As for you, he nodded his head in Tess's direction, do not date any of my detectives, I want all concentration on the job, I expect to see you both again in 15 minutes for the briefing." With that he turned on his heel and burst out of the door.

Tess felt her cheeks turn to fire, and it was nothing to do with the lack of air conditioning in this pit. She cleared her throat, was about to speak but she had no words, she looked at David in astonishment then managed to splutter.

"Did he actually just fucking say that," she blew her cheeks out. David shook his head angrily.

"Never in my life have I been so insulted. Even worse, what he said to you, what a prick, a dinosaur. Will you be OK Tess?"

"Oh I have been through much worse than that Neanderthal can dish out, believe me. So I say we go back into the briefing our academic heads held high and neither of us stoop to his level. There's a skeleton out there and we need to get answers from it. Agreed?"

David smiled; she had so many great qualities. "Agreed"
They walked back into the briefing, sat next to one another and listened to the dinosaur. During the briefing they heard about the farmer starting to put posts in his field to separate some of his animals. He had dug down to about 3 feet and came across what he thought was an animal bone, well it was, but that wasn't all. When he uncovered a human hand he called the police.

The Dig: England

They drove south from Glasgow towards Carlisle. They passed tenement buildings all separated into flats with large communal gardens extending that extended the back, Tess imagined the communal stairways, maybe with old flooring and beautiful traditional tiles? Tess loved anything antique or old. Then came the housing schemes with their grey, damp exteriors and matching match box houses, toys had been abandoned by children and littered the pavements. This reminded Tess of the council estate she had grew up on near Leeds, though her house had bordered farmland and the green and pleasant lands between Leeds and York, she would spend endless summers playing in those fields, going home smelling of long-grass, cuts to her knees where she had stumbled, daisy chain round her head, before, before it all started.

She glanced up and shook herself out of her daydream and now she saw Munros and pine forests giving way to more genteel rolling hills and single storey stone cottages. The land for a while along the borders seemed to tame, flatten near Gretna Green and beyond, then as you headed for Carlisle the dramatic atmospheric hills descended upon you, the lakes nestled between the steep hills, cloud low, most likely raining.

They headed through the village of Sawrey, Tess recalled this was where the cottage Beatrix Potter had lived in was located, she wished they had time for a bit of sightseeing. She would come back this summer if she got chance. They came to a beautiful stone farm house, pulled into the drive alongside police vehicles, some marked others not. DI dick as Tess liked to think of him stood on the drive, talking to the farmer, he had had his fair hair cropped, it made him look like fucking action man. She detested him, or did she? Oh no! She fancied him, oh fuck off she told herself, get a grip Tess.

David and Tess introduced themselves to the farmer, he was genuinely nice which was unusual as farmers normally hated archaeologists; it had been known for farmers to uncover archaeological sites in their fields and hurriedly cover them back over again. To be fair archaeological sites do become intrusive, You have the vehicles coming and going, the people and this could go on for years and years. The farmers lost the use of the land from the moment they uncovered anything, plus lots of archaeologists would rather crap behind a bush than a portaloo, hell Tess had done it often enough.

"This is like a nightmare, I can't sleep thinking of that poor person in my field, and my wife's gone to stay with our daughter while this all goes on. I mean I've walked over that place countless times, I've been walking over someone's grave. Come I'll show you, then we can have a cuppa I think we will all need it."

He showed them past the farmhouse, a beautiful pink rose grew up round a pergola just before the farmhouse door. It smelled divine, Tess inhaled as they walked past it. They climbed a sty, and crossed a field that had dried out somewhat in the sun. Chestnut and Birch trees surrounded the field, with the stunning hilly background like something from a painting. Some sort of wildflowers were growing in the shade of the trees, blue, yellow, purple and red, someone else's heaven had certainly become someone's version of hell.

Of course DI Dick had taken the lead with the farmer, they waited at blue and white police tape. A tent stood in the middle of the police cordon, these were used partly to preserve the site from rain, prying eyes, out of respect and to save sensitive souls from seeing things they would never forget. Tess and David put on white overalls and bootees. They entered the tent that had covered the grave, both to protect the site and from preying eyes too. Forgetting the archaeological arguments for and against covering skeletons, after all this was a criminal investigation. Usually as an archaeologist when a skeleton is uncovered sealing it or leaving it in view of the public is a quite different and confusing story as England and Scotland both do it differently. She thought for a moment of the implications if a skeleton was found lying across the border, what the fuck would happen then she had never come across this situation but hey you never know. First they photographed the scene as it was. Everything would remain in situ until they had devised a plan together. They asked the police to temporarily take down the tent covering the grave, they needed to use the drone to see if any other land nearby had been disturbed, they would also do a walk over the land but their naked eye might miss something the drone would pick up. David would control and fly the drone.

He set up the drone and it took off into the sky. Once finished the police quickly erected the tent again, then Tess started drawing the burial site, they would periodically draw the site at many stages of the excavation. They both had to do the work traditionally that archaeologists do but also as forensics for the police investigation. They chatted away and took notes, the grave lay east-west. They made cuts in the soil then Tess started using her leaf trowel to carefully move the soil away, they would take it in turns and methodically removed some of the soil to get an idea of what they had to work with. The soil they removed would go into labelled bags, they would look at soil analysis and anything they could gain evidence from would be logged and kept. The skull had been placed between the victims legs, this was mostly seen in some Roman burials. She and David let out a breath, she glanced at David and raised her eyebrows, He took off his glasses wiped them on his shirt then put them back on.

This was weird, it was obviously a very recent burial, yet had all the hallmarks of an ancient one. It was perplexing albeit exceptionally interesting. She carefully brushed soil from the bones as she went, she and David preferred to work alone at this point, partly so they could think and not be interrupted. When they came to where the pelvis was they both exhaled, Tess sat back and rested on her heels. David let out a whistle.

"What the hell, Tess, what the hell?"

The Artist And His Muse

He was been really kind now, maybe he was just one of those artistic weirdos, harmless just weird. He brought her to a stunning room, a dining room but much grander. A fire roared in a huge open fireplace, everything was antique and expensive. Flags hung from the walls alongside stag and bear heads. She didn't know what country the flags represented. They weren't English, Scottish or Welsh she knew that. She sat at the huge wooden table and was relieved to see a banquet of food laid out.

"Eat, you look stunning, I'm glad you wore the dress I laid out for you," he leaned over and kissed her head.

She stifled a giggle. The dress, styled like something from the Roman or Greek era. She didn't know much about history it wasn't her thing. She wondered though if this was how the other halves lived, dressing up for dinner? She had seen a cruise ship series on TV and travellers wore ball gowns and black tie for dinner. She much preferred jeans or if she was going out something skimpy that complemented her jaw dropping figure. This felt like some sort of ancient wedding gown, but hey it was still a nice thing to do.

He had a plate filled with chicken, beef and all the veg trimmings you might eat at Christmas. He motioned for her to fill her plate. She took potatoes, smoked fish and cabbage, a strange combination, though she wasn't really concentrating on the food, more him. She listened to him talking about burials? Ancient burials which is what the painting of her was based on. Normally she would be just interested in pop culture and fashion magazines. However, she found herself listening to him, he was fascinating really, especially in comparison to boys her age. Earlier she couldn't find her phone so she asked him if he had it. He said she didn't need it here, that she must've lost it although gave her another much more expensive phone.

She looked up and smiled when he kissed her head.

"It is bedtime now, muse," he said as he walked around the table and took her hand. He led her to a bedroom chamber. A huge four poster bed took centre stage. Pictures hung from the walls, or photos she wasn't too sure, they looked like burial sites or burials. Burning Viking ships with the dead laid out. Roman burials with their skeletons altered. Animal bones where human bones should be. She shuddered, thinking about his painting of her laid out on a swan wing. His dead swan he called it. She would play his dying swan, if that was his fantasy. She had been here a few weeks now; they had started sleeping together recently. He told her he loved her that she should move in and not to bother with contraceptives. She had yearned to be a mother even at her early age, maybe as she had no real family of her own. She could actually envisage herself becoming Lady to his Lord.

The Roman Way

As if the skull lying between the legs of the skeleton was distasteful, that was nothing in comparison to what they had just uncovered. Where the pelvis laid and once the womb that had been the life source of this female remained two little fragile foetus.

Tess grimaced and looked at David, he had recognition in his expression alongside sadness.

"I've seen this before Tess." He rubbed his brow deep in thought.

"OK," she replied, "I have heard and read journal articles about it, though never actually excavated one before. The disarticulation, yes but not foetuses." David nodded and they returned to their silent roles working. It was a sombre affair, for they knew this female had once been a human, now she would just be a number of bagged bones. Once excavated they would lay her on an examination table and put her bones back in order again. The thought of her being pregnant just reiterated how human she had once been.

They had already determined that the soil and burial were recent, so this would be treated as a modern crime. Having studied the skull and pubic bones they concluded what they already really knew; it was female. More answers would come in the lab. Tess turned to David and smiled, they looked at one another and exchanged knowledge, for their vocation gave them so much pleasure it was immeasurable. She felt excited about this excavation, albeit also sad. Some female had died; this was her final resting place. They had to respect that. All they could do now for this person was help the police identify her thus possibly tracking down family and friends. If the police got a conviction that stemmed from some of their work they could at least let the girl rest in peace and give some closure.

They took it in turns to excavate, the grave wasn't so big so they had placed a board over the grave cut so not to stand on the skeleton and break any bones. Tess wore knee pads to save her own bones from the excruciating pain that excavating can have on your own body. Normally they would excavate in order, from the skull, neck, torso, arms and legs then hands and feet. Though with the skull between the legs obviously the excavation and order would be a little out of their normal sequence. The body had been interred in the flexed position. Tess noted that as maybe important as in historic rural burials, they are often laid in certain ways. Extended supine, which is on its back, arms down by its side. Extended prone, which is on its face but same extension. Flexed, on its side with knees slightly bent. Crouched, on its side in a crouching or foetal type position.

"We have to be really careful with this skull Tess," David said, leaning back on his heels.

Tess made an incision through the soil below the jaw and deep to the back of the skull, that is how they would lift it. She wouldn't remove any soil from nasal aperture (nose), auditory meatus (ear) or mandible (lower jaw). Doing so could damage small bone or cartilage and the pathologist would also want their pound of flesh, pardon the pun. There were so many other professionals involved in this it was complex. David noted an animal bone in the surrounding area, they would lift this and radio carbon date to see if it matched the period of the skeleton, but most likely came from back-filling when the perpetrator dug over the grave. In other words it was most likely already in the soil and not part of the investigation, just the bones of an animal from unrelated circumstances. So often in ancient burials you would have animal bones placed where human ones should've been and animal bones that just happened to be there, more than likely the unqualified naked eye wouldn't notice or acknowledge the importance of the differences. David had taken over excavating for a while, his trowel uncovered a box. It was antique but not ancient; maybe 100 years old, Tess drew a sketch of it, detailing the Celtic cross that had been carved into the wood beautifully. David very carefully opened it. It had a red silk lining a dark blood red, on top of the lining lay a small dagger encrusted with jewels, it was smeared in blood. There was an earring just one small pearl one. A very delicate unused artists paintbrush, some dried out flowers, like they had once been a bunch, and a lock of blonde hair, the blonde hair shocked her, for she could resonate. Grave goods! That's the terminology that archaeologists used to describe goods accompanying a burial. The theories and there were countless, were these were offerings to the gods. Both in the burials of loved ones . . . and also sacrifices.

They drove back to their digs in silence, neither feeling the need for small talk. They would have something to eat and drink then retire for the night, as they had so much lab and police work to do in the morning.

They found a lovely country pub, the travellers Inn, very apt, which would make a great visit in winter; it had a huge open fire and beams. With it being summer however, hanging baskets hung outside from its walls in abundance, cascading begonias, lobelia, petunias spilled over their containers, trailing down the walls. Bees and wasps buzzed at the flowers, taking their pollen greedily. They crouched lower as they entered an olde doorway not built for their height, a passion flower and honeysuckle arch created an almost wedding entrance to the pub, the delicate scent of the honeysuckle tickling your nostrils as you entered, then the heavy smell of fermented alcohol at the pub bar. Tess was in bliss.

She took a seat overlooking a field, the field was filled with sheep drinking from a cute little stream or eating grass. David ordered her a pint of bitter and himself a white wine. She drank greedily, the heaven of bitter cooling her throat.

"I would've ordered you the barrel Tess, had I known you would gulp it so quickly," David winked as he said this cheekily.

"I am sorry I am not as refined as you David." She smiled as she wiped froth from her upper lip. They ordered food, he pork pie and peas her vegan pie and peas, they were famished after their long journey and long day in the field. David retired to his room as did Tess.

She showered undressed, put on t-shirt and shorts, it was really hot this evening. She poured herself a glass of water and got into bed then turned off the lamp. Her phone pinged; she wasn't going to check it thinking maybe it's just Jinty checking she was ok or moaning about her kids. She grabbed her phone, hell we all know what it's like to try ignoring it . . . torture. She looked at her messages, nothing so checked her email as it had the same notification sound. A sender's address she didn't recognise had emailed but she clicked the email anyhow.

Tess. How the drip drip drip scared you at the time. Does it still haunt you?

Tess went cold, literally and started to shake, then hyperventilate. She tried to breath slowly it wasn't working. Tears fell from her eyes like a violent waterfall. She put her head between her legs and tried to control her breathing. Everything came flooding back, she tried to keep those memories and thoughts at arm's length, she had to push those thoughts away right now. She was shaking even though the temperature was about 28 degrees, sweat poured from every pore she had. She called the only person she could.

Jinty's phone vibrated on her bedside table, she kept it on vibrate not to wake her devil children, Christ it had taken 2 hours to get them all down. She looked at the screen then answered so quickly she would've made a great 999 responder. It was Tess.

"Jinty, oh my God Jinty, I think it's him." Tess pulled the duvet around her chin, more as a protective blanket.

Jinty sat up and turned on the bedside light, her hubby moaning about it as she did. "Hod yae weesht you" she said as she prodded him.

"Tess, what the fuck is going on? Are you safe?" Jinty rubbed the weariness from her eyes. Wishing she hadn't when she saw the mess of her bedroom.

"Yes. No. I don't know Jinty, I have received an email and the content I have told only to you, my parents, my councillor, he knew the dripping noise petrified me?" No one else knows my thoughts, feelings and terror."

"Ok you need to give this the police, Tess this is worrying, and when are you back in Glasgow?"

Tess took a deep breath calming herself. "I should be back in a couple of days depending how far we get with this enquiry" then took a sip of water.

"Right, I will meet up with you when you get back, in the meantime I think you should ask the police you're working for to take a look?"

"Oh Jinty, the cop in charge is a complete dick, not sure about that."

"But he has a really good track record doesn't he? Forget you don't like him just remember he is good at his job, ok call him now." Tess agreed a little hesitantly but called him if under duress.

Patrick's phone cried out, he pushed the woman from the top of him, she was furious. He shushed her to be quiet. He didn't give a rat's arse about her; she was just someone he pulled last night, nothing special, a bit dumb, not the girl you would take home to your mother. He turned away from her and answered his phone.

"Hi, I am sorry to bother you, it's Dr O'Brien."

"Oh Tess," he interrupted, "have you any updates for me?"

"No, not at the moment, this was well, a different kind of call. Could you meet me? I am at the chapel air B&B," her voice faltered.

"Yes, give me half an hour I know where that is, see you soon." He smirked, was this a booty call, I mean what's a different kind of call if it's nothing to do with the case? Here he was thinking she was uptight. He told the woman to get dressed, he couldn't recall her name not that that mattered to him. He called her taxi and ushered her out of his house, with as much respect you would give to a rat that had infested your property.

The Artist And His Muse

The artist instructed the muse to lie on the four poster bed, she didn't argue and she felt a little light headed from the wine. She lay on the bed hoping sleep would envelope her, the bedding so exquisite and luxurious. She sank deep into to the Ida down, not really noticing the ropes being tied around her wrists and ankles. His art was pioneering; on completion it would almost scream torture, the last breath then death. His artwork would pulsate unlike the dead heart of his muse.

He took his easel and began to paint the scene. However, the last scene was his real pleasure, the muse's burial, now that really was his artwork at its best. He spun round and clapped his hands, applauding himself, his genius. He strode to the edge of the bed, bent down and kissed the muse on her beautiful lips; he inhaled her scent, and then went back to painting her. He had drugged her wine to make her more pliable. He sighed, he was not sure he could get the correct artistic influence and expression from her while drugged, he would leave her be for tonight. He could only ever get the painting right when his muses were dead. Alas he would have to be patient that moment would come. He left the room and strode down the beautiful sweeping staircase, took a key from his pocket and entered his favourite room in this vast house. There were rows and rows of boxes that held precious zoo archaeology artefacts. There were far too many to go through so in his time collecting them he had clearly labelled the boxes.

He looked at the box containing the wings of a swan. He took the faunal remains from the box and carefully laid them on a steel examining table. He was thinking about how he would lay them out, would he be using a full faunal skeleton or just parts? He had an easel and paper down here so he started to sketch his ideas. His muse should be grateful to him, she would be famous in death. He looked up at the ceiling of this grand room. I mean this was what it all meant, the art, the burials, the disarticulation. His eyes swept from left to right taking in the arrangement of human skeletons to create the ceiling. At the highest point of the roof, skulls had been placed in the centre, then long bones after that, then a row of skulls, then rib bones. It was an amazing fete of art and architecture. When you looked up it took your breath away. Thousands and thousands of skeleton remains made this sceptical and he was adding to it. Oh, it wasn't as grand as the Sedlec Ossuary the Czech town of Kutná Hora, where the insides of this chapel reveal skeleton chandeliers, candelabras and chalices. However he was on his way to creating something just as beautiful. The artist had already created his own chandelier; though small it hung from his centrepiece of skulls and ordered your attention like the lead actors in theatre. The drama, the theatrical and sombre nature drew you in. Long rusty chains had, had long bones attached to them draping down intermingled with candles. The chandelier was stunningly beautiful, chilling and expressive at the same time. He was talented.

Don't Go Down The Rabbit Hole Tess

Tess shut the door on her thoughts and opened the door of her air B&B to Patrick.

"Hey, what's up?" he asked as he strode into the lounge.

Tess held back tears; she didn't want him to see her weak.

"I need a confidant, but I need to be able to trust you in a professional and personal capacity?"

He frowned, and looked at her, into her soul Tess thought.

"Have you anything to drink? A beer or wine?"

"Yes, one minute, dry white wine OK?"

She entered the kitchen took a wine from the holder and poured 2 glasses, she needed this. She handed Patrick his glass, his fingers touched hers, she wasn't sure if that was deliberate or not, yet she liked it.

"Aye, cheers. So how can I help?"

She didn't understand her feelings. She didn't like this man, yet she felt very at ease blurting out her traumatic past. She told him everything, her kidnap, her families move to London after that to try put distance between what happened. She left out that her odd interest in archaeology was actually sparked by her captor's tales of burials. Her ex cheating, why did she mention that she thought. Patrick sat there and just listened. His only interruption was a nod of his head or an exhale of breath. She finished her story.

"I'll need access to your email account so I can get the tech guys to see if they can trace that email address. I don't want you telling anyone else either; the less people know the better. I will arrange a look out for your protection too."

"Thank you, but I really don't need protection, my dog killed him." She gulped wine greedily.

"What? How? Look, tell me when you are ready! But someone knows your history and has sent those emails. I am in charge it's not your decision to make Tess, this is my professional opinion we play by my rules. Aye?"
His response was quite forceful she thought, then again this is his job, she just felt a little foolish taking protection when there must be countless other Women and Men who needed it more than she.

"Have you anything in to eat, I am famished," he smiled.

"Are you not heading home? It's late," she replied. She did have food in as she had had an online shop delivered but didn't want to encourage him.

"I have had wine so can't drive, I also think it's better I sleep on your couch until we get protection for you. Just dig out a spare pillow and blanket maybe?" Although much better if he slept in her bed. He tried to banish that thought and keep professional. That was difficult, she was absolutely stunning plus so intelligent which he found more than alluring. He also felt protective of her, but she was annoying too and a feckin' vegan.

"Is that a good idea?" she queried.

She really didn't like most of his personality, yet found his arrogance and confidence very attractive. Yes Tess, hasn't that been your problem in life, going for the wrong men? She tried to shake the attractive thought out of her mind and body, you're a fucking idiot Tess, take a cold shower.

"OK, yes I get it. I will make supper and get your couch sorted, I'm not making anything too fancy, it's late." she headed to the kitchen first to rustle up a veggie sausage sarnie, and then found a spare blanket and cushions in the bedroom wardrobe.

She said night and headed to bed. Getting to sleep was difficult, she kept thinking of her life leading up to her kidnap. Part of her mind was telling her not to enter the rabbit hole, for it was dark and full of doors best left closed. She ignored that voice and ventured down the dark abyss that was her past. Summer had started off glorious, she had turned 13 and life seemed full of hope and promise. Tess was blossoming into a beautiful young woman, although she didn't let her beauty spoil her. Some so beautiful might be with the popular crowd, not Tess. She loved her weird circle of nerdy intellectual friends. It was 2007, her and her friends listened to *Nirvana*, the Cure, *the Cult*. Any type of alternative or grunge music and stuff their parents might've played. They would sit in her bedroom and blast music, eat pizza and talk about politics, their future, what they would study once at Uni.

She lived on the very outskirts of Leeds, more in the country side heading towards York. Her Dad came down south from Glasgow looking for work and met her mum in Leeds, so they had stayed there. However they always travelled to Scotland for their summer holidays. Nothing fancy, sometimes a caravan or even camping weather permitting. They spent lots of time on the West Coast, outdoor fires and keeping the midges at bay. Stories of possible relics from the Knights Templar hidden in Argyll and Bute, Monoliths erected by our Neolithic ancestor's, and the Holy Loch and Kilmun Church, said to be where Christianity came into Scotland. They would borrow her dads friends little boat, take it to little islands in the middle of vast lochs and have a picnic. Nothing extravagant or too expensive, just a love of history and the great outdoors.

Tess bolted upright in bed, something in her memories. They had taken a trip to a castle, an aristocrat's castle. It was stunning, with a backdrop of the wild highlands. Her parents had paid to view as Tess really wanted to go inside. She had a massive interest in history, although her dad always said don't believe all the hype you get taught in school. He taught her the Scottish side, the clearances, invasion and devastation. They were at the end of their visit to the castle, a tour guide had shown them round and given the history and storytelling. They were on the point of leaving when the owner and aristocrat bumped into them. He was attentive, he asked if they would like a private tour of the castle. That some things were out of the public eye. He said he could see how interested Tess was and actively encouraged youngsters to get involved with history. Tess loved it. They went into the depths of the castle normally shut off to visitors. She couldn't recall the aristocrat's name, but he showed Tess and her parents rooms that people never got to see. The ostentatious nature of the rooms although grand reinforced Tess's anger at the poor being cleared from their tiny crofts. Some doors were locked and they were not invited to enter. It reminded her of the rabbit hole in *Alice in Wonderland*.

Something about the aristocrat unnerved Tess, but she didn't know why? She was now going back in time and opening those doors. Be cautious Tess, be cautious. She opened one of the doors, it was unlocked. She entered with caution, in it she found herself laughing and running through the flat beautiful fields where she lived. The sky was brilliant blue and the rape seed fields a stunning yellow, the contrast held such beauty. Her dog was an Am staff, American Staffordshire, he was called Jude and very loyal. Like all bull breeds he was such a big softy yet would fiercely defend his owner. She lost sight of him in the tall rape seed. She called him a little anxious, it wasn't like him not to come back. She heard rustling and felt relief that Jude was heading back to her, then a hand grabbed her waist, while the other her mouth and nose. Oh fuck, and just like that she was 13 again, she would endure what no child or person should, abracadabra her childhood was gone. Her exhausted mind fought sleep, but she finally succumbed. She dreamed of her dog.

Tess woke bleary eyed from her dreams and wine consumption. She headed straight for the bathroom. She needed to pee and shower. She flung open the door to see Patrick standing there, just a towel covering his modesty.
"Oh, my fuck, I'm so sorry," she said as she shut the door. She was flustered; she thought she heard him laugh. God he was very well gym toned. She shook her head again trying to banish these thoughts. She headed downstairs and made herself a large fresh cafetière of strong coffee. Patrick came into the kitchen where Tess was sat at the table. She was pretending to read something to spare her embarrassment.

"Did you get a good eyeful, Tess? You should've come in a minute sooner, you would've seen a whole lot more," he winked and chuckled.

She was fucking furious. Who did he think he was? She was vulnerable and here he was making a joke, no understanding of her alarm or triggers.

"First of all, you will not spend another night here; I would rather risk my tormentor than have you in my house! Second, you think you are all that tasty? Fuck off and get yourself on Tinder. Now get out," she said as she strode angrily to the door and held it open for him.

"What, not even a breakfast or tattie scone roll? Shame on you, Tess. I'll get back up to protect you," he said as he left.

She picked up her trainer and threw it at the closed door. "Fucking prick." She had a pee, dressed then took a run. She was out an hour, returned to the Air B& B and showered. She had Avocado on toast with tea. She felt ready to face the world now. She texted David, they would resume their excavation/exhumation. They had a lot to do.

They headed to the police station. David noted Tess's mood. She wasn't really chatty, no small talk no professional talk either. They drove to their destination in silence. Before they entered David pulled Tess to one side.

"Everything Ok Tess? You're unusually quiet?" he looked concerned.

"Not really David, but we need to try crack this case, I don't want my personal issues interfering." She opened the door and they headed to their police meeting.

She walked in to see Patrick stood there all confidant and masculine. She sat at the back; she didn't want to feel vulnerable in the front seats. He didn't even acknowledge her, just stated he was starting the meeting. He started the meeting talking about the site, and the archaeologists input into such burials as well as their notes about the skeleton they exhumed. He mentioned both her and David's expertise in the field and gave them a nod professionally. Tess just threw Patrick a look of contempt. After the meeting David joined Patrick in discussion about the case. Tess wondered off to the canteen to grab something to drink. She entered the café and ordered a black strong tea, found a table near the window and sat down. She was thinking about the case, but also how it was similar to her own kidnap. She had yet to inform David of the significant similarity. She felt like a bit of a fraud, she should've told him when he offered her the job. On the other hand how, many others have to inform their employer about the traumas of their past. She didn't think it was important at all, at the time. However, now her past seemed to be closing in on her.

She felt a presence, and someone sat beside her, she thought it would be David, her colleague and mentor. She was shocked to see Patrick sitting there.

"I'm sorry Tess, I behaved appallingly," he rested his chin on his fist.

Tess shifted in her chair, having him apologise wasn't something she expected. She took a deep breath.

"I don't have the luxury of always having a laugh or even innocent innuendos. Someone took that away from me when I was just 13. I'm not stuck up or anything just very fearful of normal situations, I can't ever be normal and that hurts," she laid her head in her hands fighting tears.

She thought back as didn't want to share these dark thoughts. When other girls were just being that girls, finding themselves having their first boyfriend and innocent kiss. She had been denied all that, that first innocent kiss had been a grown man forcefully kissing her. She hadn't had a first fumble; a man maybe twice her age had brutally raped her. She didn't have the skills other women had. They may be learned along the way. She had grown up overnight in a horror movie. God, Patrick was starting to feel for this woman, not only her beauty but everything, her vulnerability too. He looked at her intently

"God Tess, you're something else," he squeezed her hand lightly. Just enough to let her know he cared not enough to be intrusive. She looked at him, for the first time she really looked at him. She found depth which she had not seen or noticed before.

"If you want to know me Patrick then tell me about you." She wanted not only his body but his mind and soul too.

"Let's get our working day done, then we will talk," he smiled at her and walked towards is colleagues.

Tess left the cafeteria joined David and headed for the car.

"You seem a little happier Tess," David remarked

"I guess so David. I didn't get great sleep last night so little tired."

They drove towards the site in silence. Sometimes it was a suitable time to get your working head on. They arrived at the farm and headed straight for the burial area. Typical English summer, it had gone from sweltering heat to massive downpour. Tess put up the hood on her raincoat, put her chin down and carried on walking. The police had erected a tent in which they could congregate, a little shelter for their meetings. A table had been laid out with a hot water urn, tea, coffee, milk, sugar and sweeteners. David poured out a black coffee for Tess and Milky tea with 3 sugars for himself. He handed Tess her mug which she clutched like a child clutches its favourite teddy. Patrick stood with his colleagues and nodded for Tess or David to speak. Tess stepped forward commanding an audience.

"So, the burial has hallmarks of how some Roman graves were excavated. Disarticulation, bones, skulls etc placed in various places. This is seen sometimes throughout time at different burial sites. Not just Roman. Interestingly some skeleton remains were not human, again this has been seen in historic archaeological digs. In this case we have 3 Deer ribs replacing 3 human ones. We also did a check of the area using the archaeology data service. 1 mile to the west of the body is a Monolithic structure, or a standing stone, this could be a coincidence or planned. Perpetrator has some knowledge of ancient burials at the least. Any questions?"

A detective who looked about 19 raised his hand. Tess pointed and said, "Yes"?

"Hi, Detective Braxton. Not being funny, but really?" He stifled a laugh

Tess looked at him. "Really" she said without any other explanation.

Patrick stepped forward, he threw the young detective a look. The detective looked down at his own shoes, anywhere but other people's eyes. Patrick cleared his throat and commanded the room's attention; he didn't need to ask for your attention you just gave it.

"Both these people are doctors in their field. You will respect their findings, of course you can disagree or challenge them but with a serious argument or debate. Not simply because you don't understand their field or haven't even bothered to google it!" He looked at Detective Braxton. The poor man couldn't look more uncomfortable if he tried. He looked at both Tess and David.

"I thank you for your input and academic support. I need anything you can think of as to why a murderer would bury someone this way, any interpretation you can think of or any similar cases you may have come across" he noted Tess's change in demeanour. He pulled Tess to one side.

"I need to speak with you, I've booked a table at the Indian Recluse for 19:30, see you there," he didn't wait for a response just walked off and joined his colleagues.

Tess had opened her mouth to answer, she felt like a goldfish, opening and closing her mouth with nothing coming out, and like everyone was watching her, no escape a goldfish bowl. She arrived at the curry house on time. She had never ever had to change outfits so much, she was indecisive. It was both a personal and professional meeting, but she didn't want to appear too casual, work like or sexy. She opted for blue retro Levi jeans that clung to her long legs. Brown strappy flat sandals, blue and white pinstripe shirt, opened to the start of her cleavage and tucked into her jeans, brown belt and brown bag finished her outfit. She piled her long blonde locks in a high ponytail and wore minimal makeup. She walked into the restaurant not realising every man and most women had thrown her a glance at least. She clocked Patrick at the bar and strode over to him, held out her hand in a very formal greeting. He grabbed her hand, pulled her to him and kissed her cheek. Oh the absolute arrogance, she thought, but couldn't help a wee smile, nor did she pull away. He gestured to a table for 2 in the corner of the restaurant. Indian music played quietly in the background, sounded like a love song, the man sounded all serious, the woman sounded like she was reprimanding him. They were shown to their table by a young good looking young Indian man, he kept glancing at Tess then he would blush and look away. He was very attentive, although Tess summarised if she hadn't been present, he might not have gave a shit. Menus had been placed on their table. They said nothing to one another but read the menus.

"Ready to order," Patrick queried.

"Absolutely, Indian cuisine is my favourite," Tess felt her was salivating at the thought of food.

Patrick ordered chicken pakora, very Scottish Tess thought. Tess ordered Onion Bhaji with mint vegan yogurt. They also ordered 2 bottles of white wine, house. They drank a little wine while waiting for their starter and the conversation began to flow. Patrick was wearing a white t-shirt and it clung to his biceps, Tess tried not to stare. Patrick was trying not to stare; it was like some crap game. Tess stood up to excuse herself for the loo. Patrick just stared as she sauntered through the restaurant. How could anyone be so sexy going to the loo? Tess came back and sat down.

"So, what has this case got to do with you Tess?"

She was a bit taken back; she hadn't confessed she thought it was anything to do with her kidnap.

"I noticed your body language today when we had our meeting. I'm pretty good at observing and analysing people, it's my job." He poured them more wine.

Tess picked up an onion Bhaji took a bite then a big sip of wine. She explained, she didn't understand the threatening emails, there were things only the kidnapper would know, and how would he have got her personal email anyhow? This case was really unnerving her. There were things that her captor had said that resonated with the burial of this woman, but she couldn't remember, or maybe she could if she tried. Don't go down the rabbit hole Tess, don't open those doors. Patrick looked at her intensively.

"I've had a quick look at your case Tess, certain details I'm not keen on, they don't add up. I have requested that it be opened again, I need to compare every detail, something is missing, and I want to find out exactly what it is. Tess, do you feel like all the loose ends were tied up. Do you feel like they missed something?"

He picked at his pakora then dipped it in the bright red sauce that accompanied it. Pain etched on her face; it was obvious this was going to be very ugly for her to delve into again. She blew air from her mouth and inhaled deeply.

"I remember all my life before, small parts of my kidnap, normally when I'm having nightmares then I wake up. I recall trying to kill myself aged 17; I tried to do that as I had opened some doors in my memory, and they were too painful. I wrote diaries, I have never gone back and read them, I burned them instead, I'm sorry they could've held vital information couldn't they? They might've benefited you? Especially a trained detective," she tilted her head as she looked at him.

"Nothing we can do about that now. Now let's change the subject, take some time out and enjoy our meal."

There main course arrived. Consisting of a nan bread that hung off what looked like a modern flat Christmas tree, chapattis arrived in baskets with beautiful extravagant Indian cloths covering them, both had ordered chilli garlic dishes. They chatted and laughed, Tess leant over and kissed Patrick on the lips, he was taken back. They paid the bill, he insisted on paying. They were making their way out when an angry petite woman approached Patrick.

"You fucking pig," she cried as she slapped him round the face. She didn't wait for a reply but stormed off as fast as her teetering heels could carry her. Tess looked at Patrick, sighed and ordered a cab through reception.

2007

Tess feels a little shaky, but the doctors have said she could be discharged from Leeds General Infirmary. Her mum and dad are at the foot of her bed talking to the doctor while hugging one another and crying. The doctor approaches Tess.

"You've had a very lucky escape Tess; your liver could've been damaged or worse. I will contact your doctor for further care I really think you need to speak to a professional in mental health," he nodded to her parents turned on his heels and left.

"Come on love," said her dad, "we'll call a cab." He didn't own a mobile. He searched his pockets for change.

"Where's your car dad, you haven't had a crash or anything," she felt her heart rate go up in panic.

Her mum looked at her dad. Although still beautiful and her dad handsome they had aged since the . . . well since you know what. Her mum's face lit up a little, "we've sold it Tess, and we got a few thousand for it," with that she smiled.

"You need your car dad, it's your prize possession." She was a little confused.

"No, no I don't, what we need is a holiday to Thailand, at an elephant sanctuary. If you ever feel suicidal again, I want you to think like you did last time about something in life you haven't achieved. If we have to sell the house and everything, we own to have you live, then that's exactly what we will do Tess."

Her parents grabbed her in a group hug, this was the only time she ever felt safe. God, she loved them.

2022

She was sleeping, her dream suddenly changed. Don't go down there Tess, don't go down. She was underground, large roots protruded from the ceiling and bulged underfoot. Arched wooden doorways painted assorted colours went on and on in rows, a key hung on the wall beside each door. The keys seemed extra-large and made of wrought iron. Each door had a large keyhole, yet the doors were small, things were out of proportion. She reached for the first key just as a deer ran past her, the deer seemed significant. She watched it run away, it turned to look in her direction, it had tears in its eyes, and she saw a gaping hole in its torso, she could see its ribs, well some were missing, the deer vanished. Should she chase it? Was that part of the game? She dares not Instead she put the key in the lock of the door, it unlocked with a moan and creak. She took a breath and turned the handle pushing the door so very slowly. Inside she could see herself and her friends, they were in her bedroom playing the cure laughing and joking about something. She recalled they were excited about going on a school trip the next week to the natural museum in London. The doorbell rang and Tess left her friends and headed to answer it. A man stood outside with a package. She didn't take much notice of him really; she wanted to get back to her friends.

"I have a package for your parents, are they in? I can't leave it with an underage."

"No sorry they're out, I'll tell them you stopped by," she tilted her head to one side and threw back her long blond hair. Out of nowhere her Am staff Jude appeared, he rarely barked but people felt his muscly presence. Jude's hackles went up, he stepped forward growled, his massive jaw like a sharks. She grabbed his collar.

"Jude," she giggled, "you can be so naughty." She was trying to chastise him but that was impossible, she kissed his huge head.

"I'm very sorry. I don't know what gets into him sometimes.

The man backed off raising his hands. "Don't tell your parents as this is a surprise gift, will they be home later?" Fucking dog was nuts and huge.

"Not until after 9, they are visiting my gran in hospital, it's in York so a bit of a drive. Bye," with that she shut the door.

Tess tried to view the man's face, but couldn't see it, she tried she really did. Then a rabbit appeared, everything else disappeared. It was cartoon like wore glasses and a dark red smoking jacket from a vintage shop. It lit up a cigar. A swan was visible in the background, it only had one wing, and it looked at her sadly.

The rabbit spoke, "You have to open these doors Tess, all of them to make sense."

Something about the rabbit was familiar but she didn't know what. Then Tess could feel herself being pulled backwards, fast, the rabbit hole swirling about her. Tess woke up with a start, she was sweating and breathing hard. She looked at her phone, 5am. She had left a jotter and pen on her bedside table, she jotted down her crazy dream. Checked her phone, 2 missed calls and 3 texts from Patrick! Fuck him, she jumped out of bed, nothing better to clear her head than an early morning run, before it got busy. She was heading for the door when she stopped in her tracks. She wondered if her parents ever received that parcel? She never asked as she never got to, as that was the day of her kidnap. The man with the parcel had been far from her mind and insignificant. That day they lost their innocent teenage daughter, what came home was more like a zombie, not their care free, geeky teenager. Her parents were holidaying in Greece, these days, her dad did have a mobile phone, she called it.

It was a Saturday, Patrick was having a long lie, sometimes he didn't get weekends off especially with a murder case. Though he wasn't at work he would be working from home, calling the original investigating force, West Yorkshire police. He yawned and went back to sleep.

Tess called her parents, Tess's dad John picked up straight away. "Hey Janet, Janet, quickly it's our girl," he had beckoned Tess's mum over to the phone. They put it on loud speaker.

They both chatted at the same time. "Hi baby, everything ok? We are having olives and wine."

"Hi Mum hi Dad, yes absolutely fab, the job is going great, flat is gorgeous, and I'm fine, really." She always had to convince them, the last thing she wanted to do was worry them. She lied, she told them she was having regression therapy and the man with the parcel came up.

"So just querying if you ever got the parcel? He said he would be back later. My therapist says it's important if I remember anything to clarify if I can," She was glad it was a phone call, she couldn't lie to them face to face and they would see her anguish. Her dad was first to answer.

"No, we never got a parcel, but it was near to our anniversary so maybe someone sent something and then retracted it after the news broke."

Patrick started to read the very first statements Tess's parents gave. They along with all the statements had been sent to a very secure email by West Yorkshire Police. Her mum talked first

"We got home just after 9. She had gone but so was Jude her dog so we thought they were out walking. It got to about 9.30 and we grew concerned, we had asked her not to go out too late even with Jude. We started calling her friends, then went looking for them, that's when we found Jude, up on the farmers field lying in the rape seed, he had been bludgeoned but still breathing. That's when we knew Tess, had, oh my god."

He read on. They had called the police and their vet, the vet arriving first. Their vet Lisa had rushed Jude to the surgery, she said she would keep them informed. They both kissed and held him before he was rushed away.

The investigating officer DC Wright had been furious, he said the dog could have had evidence and shouldn't have been removed from the scene. He and the vet exchanged some strong profanities. The vet said to send forensics down, she had operated on Jude, had done all she could, now he had to fight. DC Wright sent down forensics, but anything on the dog would surely be contaminated now. Friends of Tess who had been with her on that day had said she was in good spirits, all excited about the natural history museum, apparently they would be staying overnight in the actual museum. Who knew you could do such a thing Patrick thought. His thought was interrupted by his mobile, he fucking hated those things sometimes. The call screen said Tess, he thought she would thaw eventually. She called the prick's number, purely professional. He picked up straight away. Now her run was in ruins she had made a strong coffee, expresso. She gulped the lot before speaking.

"First, I am calling you as a DI, absolutely nothing more, OK?" She had bought more fags and lit one, inhaling deeply then stuttering.

"I hear you. And a good morning to you too. Not sure how me getting fucking assaulted by a deranged female with bad hair is my fault but?" Now he was annoyed. "And are you smoking? Disgusting."

"Yes smoking and loving it, maybe I'll take it up full-time, alongside fucking lap dancing. None of your business! I want to discuss the case, my case too."

"You want to discuss the case? then we will discuss it on my terms , my terms OK!? I'm in Berwick on Tweed, River cottage. From the main street follow the wee cobbled road, can't miss it. 2pm sharp. If you don't turn up book an appointment to speak with me at the station." With that he hung up. Well as well as you can on a mobile, nothing like the old days when you slammed a phone down people new about it. Tess just stood gawping open mouthed at her phone. She was about to argue back but the twat put the phone down on her. She was absolutely raging. She had on her running gear and finally headed for the door for that long awaited run.

The Dying Swan

The Artist had been busy. He laid the swan's wing on the bed then positioned his muse draped over it. He wanted his artwork to be world renowned. The swan's wings looked stunning, but would be much better when she was nothing but bones too, that was his aim, the grand finale, the masterpiece. He stood behind his easel and began to paint; this was the final painting before death. He loved to capture every stage.

She could barely open her eyes, her head banged like a motherfucking drum at a rock concert. She tried to make sense of what was happening, she knew this was wrong to the core. A tear rolled down her cheek, not just sadness, not just loss, her loss, what could've been. She knew she was going to die, in some way it was almost a relief she had acknowledged it. Who would miss her anyhow? No parents, or family, friends from her years in care were mostly gone, drugs, prostitution, anything to blot out the pain of growing up without love. Death would be better. Yet she was angry, she had tried. She hadn't let drugs take her or prostitution. She had knuckled down at school. Not a genius but by god she had given it her all. She had got into Uni, all alone in this world yet she had done it. She was struggling to focus. She hoped it was quick. He had lied to her, the artist, promised her the good life a wealthy life, seduced her with his charm and money and even got her pregnant. All she ever longed for was a loving family to call her own. She thought she had that in her sights, but no he was going to cruelly snatch that away from her. Even worse their child would die alongside her, never to breathe air.

2007

Tess's captor was on the phone, she couldn't hear much. She wasn't sure, maybe she just imagined it. Whoever he was talking to he has lied to, big fat fucking lie. He just said he hadn't hurt her, filthy disgusting liar. If she got chance again she would bite off his ugly ear or his nose, make him pay for life like he had her. She heard that drip, drip, drip, it was as torturous as her tormentor. He strolled over to her and put a drink and sandwich at her feet. She wanted to recoil but wouldn't let him see that.

"Shove it up your ugly arse. If I'm going to die I will die on my terms only. So I'll fucking starve and dehydrate to death, you prick."

She looked up at him. He was filthy; his cheek was starting to scar from her attack even though he had crudely sown it. She sniggered at him. He couldn't hurt her more than he already had, so who fucking gave a shit anymore. Her captor spat on her then left abruptly.

The police dogs didn't seem to find a scent, well they did then it went cold. She might have been moved to a car at this point? The river Aire was also been searched as was the canal. Forensics in white overalls on hands and knees combed the area, looking for any clue to Tess's disappearance. The heat in those suits was unbearable, yet they carried on regardless of their own suffering, totally focused on finding a 13 year old girl. Tess's parents had finally been able to get Jude home, the vet had wavered her fee of over a thousand pounds. Jude was home but not himself, he kept looking for Tess.

Tess could hear that scratching again, and then a whimper, a rat shot out near her feet, she recoiled in horror. Her captor had told her Jude was dead, that he had battered him to death, that hurt Tess more than her rape and kidnap, she couldn't bare life without him. She had spent some time in a vehicle, possibly a van by the sounds it made. They arrived at her new prison, this time her captor had left off her gag, he hadn't got close enough so she could bite him, just took off the gag and left her food and water. A thought hit her, if he had left off her gag then no one could hear them, he wasn't that stupid. She was in an underground bunker or a cellar, but it was deep underground. Her thoughts turned to Jude again, if he was dead, she would have to face that and ultimately that was her responsibility, she had been responsible for Jude's care that day, it was all down to her. She was no longer shackled, that reinforced the theory no one would find her, she was somewhere isolated.

2022 Patrick

Tess drove like a maniac towards the address Patrick had given her. Another thing Tess was good at was driving. Before well you know, she had attended many rallies with her dad, he had a rally car and off they would go the two of them, always excluding her mum who seemed grateful for some alone time. They would go down to Doncaster in South Yorkshire, and Tess had driven at rallies. When her dad raced she would be screaming him on from the side-line. Sometimes he won and they always had a chip butty and tea afterwards, before driving back to Leeds. Now Tess was driving like her dad down winding country lanes, leaning into the corners as she took them, the tyres screeching in protest. As she got nearer town she slowed right down, the protection car nearly rammed her car from behind, the male police officer was shouting some obscenity in her direction. She turned round and flipped him the finger, she's sure his female colleague chuckled, the policeman then turned his anger on his female counterpart

Tess walked up to the door of River cottage, she could barely contain her contempt or anger. She nearly knocked the fucking door from its hinges. She looked around, he must rent this, he couldn't own something so quaint. The gate to the cottage led you down a winding path, French and English lavender spilling over and blurring the edges of the pathway, the scent was just out of this world, foxgloves and lupins swayed slightly in the breeze. The door was a lovely sage green, the man inside was a dick.

Patrick opened the door. The weather was hot and close, he wore shorts and a casual t-shirt. The t-shirt clung to his arms and chest, his shorts showing off his large calves. He didn't speak but beckoned Tess to come in. The aroma hit her, fresh bread and garlic first. She followed him through a short hallway, coat and umbrella stand in the corner, terracotta tiles then a staircase to the upper floor that invited you to dare climb it, it swept round, dark wood then white painted stairs. Tess imagined trying to leave quietly on a morning, and then she shoved or elbowed that thought out of her stupid head. Once in the kitchen he offered her freshly ground coffee or wine, she opted for coffee, well for now. He didn't offer an apology. He passed her black coffee without any conversation she grabbed it and stared at him, fucking furiously.

"Follow me," he said and walked towards huge bifold windows. This must've been a modern addition to the cottage and took Tess by surprise. Patrick opened the doors revealing a cute decked area that led out to the river, a small boat was docked at the bottom of the garden. It was stiflingly hot. She never uttered a word, if she had started first she would've just spewed profanities. Patrick sat on a comfy bean bag and motioned his hand for Tess to do the same. She sat and still didn't speak. Patrick let out a sigh, "So what is the issue? You see someone, rather some female hit me then deduct or decide what exactly Tess?"

"What? She was fucking furious, obviously you have hurt her in some way?"

Tess gulped the coffee, she really needed the wine now.

"Look Tess, I'm single you're single right? The night you called me about the email I was entertaining her, I'll admit that. Once I got your message I started to worry and asked her to leave, end of. I don't really owe you an explanation. We're not dating or an item, aye? You're blowing this out of proportion Tess. Anyhow, it was not ok for her to slap me in any case was it? I think we need wine."

He strode off into the kitchen to fetch wine and glasses. He came back and poured them both a pretty large glass.

"Totally agree Patrick, but why did she react so badly if you let her down gently or just said work had cropped up?"

Tess picked at her toes, not a great habit but she did so when stressed. She had worn denim shorts, flip flops and a white top that complimented her tan. Patrick had noticed, oh boy had he noticed. She had plaited her hair, mostly to keep the sweat away from her hairline, minimal make-up, just a lip gloss and mascara.

Patrick looked at her his gaze intense. "Ok, I dropped her like a stone because you messaged me, not proud or a nice chivalry thing to do but hey, there you have it the truth."

At that moment 2 ducks hopped into the garden from the river, Patrick smiled, he fed them some bread. "Hey Tess meet Dempsey and Makepeace."

Tess didn't expect this, he was a complex character. He was intriguing her. Tess jumped up and went to meet the ducks. They drank more wine, never a good idea and chatted some more. Another shock, Patrick was a great cook, he made garlic tear and share bread from scratch, they ate it with green olives and a chilli olive oil dip.
"Is this house yours Patrick? it's not what I expected, I was thinking a modern apartment or something." She dipped more delicious bread into the chilli oil.

Patrick raised his eyebrows in a mock surprised look and then looked a little sad.

"My gran's from here, this was hers. I'm not really here on a permanent basis, I'm based in Glasgow but they needed a decent DI and they chose me. I thought with Gran so old I could help take care of her and work at the same time. It was fantastic while it lasted but she passed away a few months ago, left me the house bless her. That's not the reason I moved in with her, I didn't expect anything from her. Oh and she's also the reason I'm a fantastic cook, she taught me everything," he smiled reminiscing.

Tess thought for a moment. Was all the bravado an act? He had more layers to him than an onion, some rotten and some so good. Tess leaned over and kissed Patrick full on the lips, she pulled away slightly, he held the back of her head but left it to her to take the lead, she grabbed his wrist and motioned him to pull her head closer to his, he didn't hesitate. God this was bliss. She was a little light headed due to the wine, but clear enough to know exactly what she was doing. They reached his bedroom, they both started stripping off with Tess getting her leg caught in her shorts, she stumbled and landed on her back. Omg nothing romantic about this moment. He asked if she was OK, when she nodded they both let out loud laughs and didn't stop until he leaned forward and kissed her passionately. They moved over to a beautiful antique sleigh bed, his gran had had good taste.

"You sure, Tess?" Patrick asked.

"Yup," she answered and that was the start of their very tumultuous journey.

She woke the next morning. She hadn't slept that good in years. Patrick was already up so she borrowed his dressing gown and made her way downstairs. He was in the kitchen stirring mushrooms in a frying pan, he heard her enter turned round and smiled. As lovely as it was, she still had a little knot in her stomach. You know when you meet someone then sleep with them for the first time there is always a little trepidation of where it is leading, if anywhere. She didn't give herself freely or easily to anyone, never had one night stands. Yet Patrick had barely had to work at all to get her.

"Morning Tess, are mushrooms on toast ok? I have some of that vegan stuff instead of butter.

"Fab, I'm famished."

He buttered toast and piled on a mix of wild mushrooms. Tess sat at the table and poured herself tea. They ate greedily, once they had finished their food Patrick spoke.

"So we have just met, but I want to see where this goes Tess, if you would like that. I think for now though we keep it to ourselves because of work and the gossips." He took a sip of tea.

"Only one problem with that detective, we both forgot about the protection car outside that's watching my every move. Oh, and he might be a bit pissed at me already" she laughed.

"Oh fuck, wait here I'll go have a word with them"
He went down the path towards the gate then bent down outside an undercover car. One male and female officer sat eating breakfast, the male opened the car window and smirked at his boss.

"Busy night sir?" He turned and looked at his female colleague who seemed more uncomfortable. Patrick reached into the car and grabbed the cheeky little twat by the throat.

"Amazing night, but I'm a grown up, as you should be, so we don't laugh and snigger and twang bra straps, OK? And we most certainly do not gossip at the station with other moronic juveniles. One word one fucking word and your career is done," with that he let go of the young lads throat.

The lad coughed, the female cop sniggered at her colleague's distress.

"Ma'am." Patrick nodded and walked off. When Patrick was a safe distance away the police officer leant out of his window and yelled.

"Hey, maybe speak to your girlfriend about her driving, next time she will get a ticket off of me, she's mental" The female officer dug him in his ribs.

"Are you on a death wish? I wouldn't mess with him he's mental, so you keep your mouth shut yeah? If you don't I'll tell the boss about you and me, me been a trainee and all, tut tut" with that she flicked down the passenger mirror re-applied her lip-gloss and tied her long auburn hair in a tight bun. "Now let me drive, you're shite" He took out the keys and threw them at her. As they swapped seats Tess came striding out of Patricks, all long legs and blond hair. She waved at the female cop then flipped her finger again at the male. The male let out a sigh. "How the fuck does Patrick even get her, she's an arse but fucking hot." The female replied quickly, "because he's also hot and all man."

Tess indicated and pulled out, waved and smiled again at the female officer. They would tail her to the station, then go home to sleep, someone else would take up this tedious duty once she went home or wherever. He had seen the police tailing Tess, that's fine and as she was busy investigating this burial in England it gave him chance to drive further north in Scotland and take a look at where she lived and worked, it would make it easier in the future. He located her flat. Pretty busy here as it's in the West End of Glasgow so very trendy and full of students. He also watched some female students, but they weren't perfect, well not like her. He would continue to study her from a distance, for now. He had studied her right from the age of 13, before the event and after it too. She would always be his perfect Muse.

Patrick had just showered and was getting ready for work when his phone rang. He swiped the answer sign and put the phone to his ear.

"Hey gorgeous."

Once he finished his call he dressed in a grey suit, no tie he couldn't conform that much, headed for his car and drove to the station. He entered the building with purpose, throwing the door open it clattered against the wall, he commanded respect. He was early so waked to his office first. He sat down and turned on his computer, did a quick recap of what he wanted to go through. His desk phone rang.

"Yes, yes, show her in please."

A gorgeous brunette entered his office, very slim and about 5 ft., 6 in. Patrick stood up and greeted her with a bear hug nearly squashing her in the process. "We will have to talk later I'm in a rush, shall I meet you back home? God I've missed you," he dazzled gorgeous white teeth.

"Yes, home will be fine I'll order a take out, see you later," she turned on her heel and blew him a kiss. Patrick winked then left the office for the meeting room.

Tess was stood at the back with her colleague David, he couldn't be bothered with all this Doctor stuff. He nodded at them both. People had been chatting quietly but most shut up now. Tess was stood behind a female DC who was whispering to her male colleague, Tess just caught, "stunning, younger in Patrick's office just now. She was escorted in like someone hot or some hot wife."

Tess felt her heart sink, what a fool Tess what a fool. She could barely concentrate on what Patrick was telling people in the conference. He tried catching her eye, she looked at her feet like a naughty school child chastised for dodging class. She was fucking raging, but she also needed to talk to her therapist, urgently. Patrick finished the meeting and Tess strode past him quickly. He went to catch her arm but she shrugged him off, maybe too aggressively considering people were watching. She had to get out of this building. It was hot and stuffy inside and she couldn't breathe, she crashed through the doors, sat on a wall by the steps to the police building and took deep steady breaths. She felt sick, she was starting to panic. All she could smell was sweat, hers or others she didn't know but it made her gag. She felt a hand on her shoulder.

"Tess, you okay?" Patrick looked at her concerned, yes right.
She rubbed her forehead, "Just leave me alone please."

He sat next to her. "I don't understand Tess, we were fine this morning. Did I overstep the mark or something?" He went to push sweaty hair from Tess's face, she slapped his hand away.

"Overstep the fucking mark, are you serious? You have another woman and you fake concern for me, fuck I feel cheap" She headed for David's battered jeep, she needed to put space in between herself and Patrick, she thought she might punch him. Thank God David started towards the jeep, clicked his car key and it beeped unlocking it. Tess jumped in and locked her door. Patrick stared at her in the distance, she could see him shrug and shake his head then head back inside that furnace of a building. David got in made pleasantries then started the car. He dropped Tess at her digs. She would call her therapist then have a long soak.

Jude

Tess's mum Janet had let Jude out for the toilet, she called him back in but there was no sign of him. Panicked she ran in and shouted for John.

Another day dawned. The police were still combing the area where Tess had been kidnapped. Some had sniffer dogs others were on hand and knee intensely searching for any clue or evidence that could help find Tess, welfare units were in abundance so forensics and police could take much needed breaks. One eagle eyed officer spotted a dog running like its life depended on it about a football fields distance away

Hey, Hey he shouted to his colleagues, isn't that Tess's dog Jude? The officer didn't wait for a reply but started chasing after Jude, he shouted and shouted!!! Occasionally Jude would wait for him to catch up but then his hackles would go up and he would run and run. The officer couldn't let him out of his sight. PC Moran was a rookie, no one really noticed him much but that was all about to change. He followed Jude into a dense copse of trees, and what seemed like a pipe outlet, some sort of old water system maybe, he had to crouch and swipe ivy and other foliage away, the foliage largely concealed the outlet. He got on his hands and knees and crawled through, it smelled foul, like sewage and rotting vegetation or worse. Jude led Pc Moran ran down into the dark bunker, following Jude's lead. He noticed the dog was struggling; he would be having been through his torment. Yet Jude was so focused on Tess's scent that he would happily die for her, his best pal in the world. The dog waited at the entrance to the bunker, looking at Moran for guidance. Moran tried the door to no avail, it seemed shut tight. He stepped back, then launched himself shoulder first at the door. It budged a little. He launched himself again! Shouting as he did! TESS! He felt the door weaken, again he shouted TESS! This time he backed right up then ran like he had never ran before, TESS! The door broke through and PC Moran landed on the floor, momentarily stunned, Jude licked the side of his face although PC Moran sensed a sadness from the dog, he knew in that instant that Tess wasn't here, he also knew she wasn't dead, otherwise Jude would've reacted differently. Moran had never experienced a dog like this one! His training with the police had been that bull breeds were dangerous, pit-bulls really. He now thought very differently, Jude's loyalty, drive, and dedication to his Tess all the while suffering serious injuries highlighted how intelligent bull breeds were and empathised emotionally. Moran tenderly kissed the dog's forehead. "We will find her Jude, alive, I promise you that'," with that He checked the bunker just in case, then radioed it in.

The Other Woman

Patrick was pissed off, but he wasn't going to let Tess ruin this for him. He stopped at the main street went into the chippy aptly named when the boat comes in. He ordered 2 fish suppers with curry sauce and scraps. Now scraps weren't something you really got in Scotland it was an English thing. If you thought about it too much they were pretty disgusting. All the batter and scraps of battered fish were scooped from the oil and that's it the dregs were scraps and served over your fish suppers. Although Patrick had succumbed to this English quirk, just like he had Tess. He had tried to be good he really had, but to no avail. Tess was just too tempting, she was alluring without meaning to be. Sexy without trying. Damaged beyond help? annoying purposely. Oh and intelligent without having to think too much. "Sir, Sir, salt and vinegar" asked the man behind the counter. Patrick had been in deep thought so not heard him. "Yes, lots on both please."

He paid the server, jumped in his car and headed home. As he opened the door she stood there in the hallway, head cocked and frowning. She held two wine glasses in her hand, looked at Patrick and raised her eyebrows.

"Dad, really? My god what woman would date you?" Gina ran forward and hugged him tightly laughing all the while. Patrick kissed the top of her head, she always had that baby smell, maybe because she was his baby. "Well we will see but she is one complicated woman, show me one that isn't." Gina fake punched her dad on his arm, then shook her fist in feigned pain. They had done this routine all her life. She was mocking his muscular frame. "Like punching a lamp-post on steroids," Patrick replied.

"Oh, speaking of steroids how's the idiot?" He couldn't really contain his contempt.

"Dad! Do you have to spoil it? Why don't you and your girlfriend come for a meal with us? Maybe she won't be as mean as you?"

Gina stood on her tiptoes and reached for the plates for the fish suppers.

"Gina, I'll eat mine out of the box thanks," he would happily go back to eating them from old newspapers, oh there's a memory, the newspaper soaking up vinegar. She pulled a grossed out face at him.
"No you won't. Gran would have had your guts," she said as she passed him a plate and they sat at the farmhouse style kitchen table. Gina had picked flowers and arranged them in a vase in the centre of the table. She was very much like her gran, lots of heart and attention to detail. Patrick poured curry sauce all over his fish and chips.

"Oh and she's not my girlfriend, not sure she is anything at all come to that," he picked a chip up with his fingers and ate it greedily. Gina punched him on the arm again. "If you eat like an animal and prefer not to use plates either, then no wonder she's not interested. What did you do to this one?" she frowned. He stifled a laugh.

"Not a thing, all good this morning when she left here, then at work nothing but the cold shoulder."

"Oh dad she stayed over! In Gran's house? Have some respect." She jumped up to put on a pot of tea. She was always like this, outspoken, cheeky, intelligent, hilariously funny, God and so beautiful. He had no idea how he had been part of her creation. He couldn't even say she was like her mother, she was nothing like her. She was all his mum, that's who he had to thank. She plonked down two cups of cafetière, added cream and sweeteners.

"I don't take sweetener, its 1 sugar, sugar," he said.

"Dad at your age you need to be careful," she giggled at her own joke. Patrick had got his high school sweetheart pregnant, he was 14 and she 17 when Gina was born. It was a private joke between him and Gina now. How young he had been. Patrick was only 36, yet had a daughter of 22. Ah he thought to himself. People often came to the wrong disgusting conclusion when seeing Gina and him together, she had been at the station today, Tess threw a fit at him. It didn't help that his colleagues at the station were gossipy as fuck.

"Gina, I really like her. What should I do?"

She winked at him "Leave it to me" with that she grabbed him and kissed his cheek. Jumped up and out of the door she went. The hurricane was her nickname.

Tess's phone was bleeping again. She didn't answer but looked at the screen. 10 missed calls from Patrick. She launched her phone across the room, luckily it landed on the other couch. She opened up her laptop, had a look through Academia for any relevant archaeological papers she could do with reading. She found an interesting one on skeletal foetuses, she bookmarked it for later. She scrolled through BADJR which was an archaeological site. She could do with an apprentice. The university had decided to take on a student from a difficult background, Tess would take her through the steps, from undergraduate right through to masters or higher.

They would have to complete a small essay, stating why they were interested and what they could potentially bring to the research department. Tess would guide them through the academic side, writing essays and completing research, but the most exciting part for any potential mentor would be the lab side, the bones, the excavation, the interpretation as to why some are buried the way they are. Disarticulation, animal bones it was just a dream job for the slightly more macabre person. She would place an advertisement this week in BADJR and also send emails out to children's homes, welfare officers and underprivileged schools. She opened a bottle of white wine, interestingly an Orkney based company, gosh Tess had had fun up in Orkney completing her PHD. She had spent the start of cool summers excavating some of Orkneys most captivating sites. From Neolithic to the Second World War. She would work as a tour guide too to earn more money. She smiled at the thought, opened up her laptop and was about to read the article on skeletal foetuses when the doorbell went.

Tess jumped up but was cautious to answer it, I mean who wouldn't be in her shoes. She peered through the keyhole. She opened the door and in wafted the smell of cut grass, rain and expensive perfume. A woman stood there, maybe 10 years younger than herself. Tess inhaled, she was utterly beautiful. Medium height with long dark cascading wavy hair, full lips and piercing blue eyes.

"Can I help you," Tess enquired.

The woman held out her hand, Tess shook it and the woman walked right into the lounge, just like that, uninvited.

"Hi I'm Gina Patrick's daughter, so good to meet you," she smiled at Tess a warm friendly smile but also something else, something behind the smile. She also had that weird accent too that was neither Scottish nor English.

"Erm, his what? Sorry how old are you." Tess was a little confused, how the fuck was this his daughter? She was well a woman and Patrick wasn't that old.

"Hey I'm 22, don't panic, dad was a bit of a bad boy at school," she laughed and stood back to take in Tess.

Well typical Patrick if nothing else Tess thought! Fucking bad boy that's for sure.

"Ok, why are you here, may I ask." Tess was totally perplexed

"Well, dad said he had met someone, which is shocking as he never really dates, just one night stands I suppose. He seemed a little upset that you'd given him the cold shoulder today. I bet it's those gossiping wankers at the cop shop, huh?" Gina wandered through the house, found the kitchen got herself a glass and poured herself some of Tess's wine. Tess stood there opening and closing her mouth like a goldfish.

"Do come in and make yourself at home! Apple doesn't fall far from the tree, hey?" Tess poured herself another glass. She thought she might need it.

"Look, don't shoot the messenger, dad doesn't know I'm here, he left his laptop open and it had your details and your temporary accommodation as a work colleague," Gina smirked.

The messenger, more like a fucking rocket Tess thought.

Tess was going to ask her if she often barged into people's places but she knew the answer to that one.

"Look I have of work to do, so how can I help?" Tess gulped wine like it was an Olympic sport.

"Work? What, bodies and stuff, it's weird," Gina sniffed the air as though she could smell death.

"Actually, skeletons and stuff! Would you like to see some?" It was Tess's time to smirk.

"Erm, no. Thank God I'm a model, couldn't be doing with no boring job," she paused for a second to check out her manicure. "Listen Jess."

"Tess," Tess interjected.

"Whatever, I would really like you to join me and dad for a meal tonight?" She jutted out her chin, smiled sweetly and fluttered her eyelashes at Tess. Tess could imagine Patrick bowing to her every whim.

Tess inhaled deeply, "why?" she asked bluntly.

"Tess, my dad has spent his life looking after me, since I was born when he was 14, can you imagine that? Mum was 17, don't think that's even legal, had me then fucked off. Nan took the role of mum and between them they raised me. Dad joined the force and just lived for me his mum and his career. He has never had a serious relationship, never had the time, oh and he can be a bit of a twat, in case you hadn't noticed?" Gina gave the most beautiful wide grin at that. "Now's his time Tess, he needs a life, maybe marriage and more kids." Gina's expression turned serious.

Tess put up her hands in a whoa motion.

"Hey! Meal first before we skip to kids, I'm not such a cheap date. You just tell me what time and where and I will book a taxi."

Tess had warmed to the girl, she was being selfless and putting others feelings first, although she was under no illusion that this could be a bumpy ride with these two.

"Great, can we say tomorrow at seven, a little Palestinian restaurant called Hebron's, Berwick? I'll book." Gina jumped up like an excited schoolgirl, smiled at Tess and hugged her. "See you tomorrow," and off she went, like a whirlwind.

Tess, waved her off, and then shook her head in disbelief. Bloody hell she was something else.

She went back to reading her academia article, then it would be shower, pyjamas and bed, she was exhausted. She sank into the comfy large bed and let her mind wonder. She was drawn down the rabbit hole once again. Was she brave enough to go there? Just one door Tess, one door that's all. She let herself go. She was underground again in that same place with roots of trees all round her and arched little doors. She stopped at a little blue door and reached for the key. She opened it cautiously and peeked inside. It felt like she was peering into a goldfish bowl. Her school friends all stood there looking at her. "Hey Tess, come on jump," they dared. They were camping with school up in the Lake District near Windermere. They had so much fun eating baked potatoes from the fire, canoeing and sailing. This time they were ghyll scrambling.

They had clambered next to a rocky fast stream and hung onto rocks as they followed the stream upwards. All the time fighting the water cascading down on their heads. Up and up they went in their helmets and bright waterproofs. They reached the top. The only way back down was to jump into a pool down a waterfall. It was high and scary. Her friends had all gone first, then when they had swam out of the pool they shouted, dared and beckoned her to jump. She didn't like heights. Yet she wasn't the type of girl to lose face. She faced her fear, held her nose and jumped. When she opened her eyes she wasn't in a pool of water. She was in a pool of her own urine. The burning sensation between her legs was agony, like someone had stabbed her with a sword. Blood was on the floor and down her legs, her virginity, innocence, and childhood gone. She wanted to be six again when she still slept between her parents, safe and loved. Yet she was in hell, a concrete hell with a monster. She mustered courage to look up. Her kidnapper and rapist sat there, casually looking at a porn magazine. She blacked out.

Tess woke sweating and shaking. She ran to the on-suite loo and threw up. When finished she sat hugging the loo, blowing air from her bottom lip towards her brow to cool down. She had never really noticed the on-suite much, now she took in every nook and cranny. Granite looking loo and basin with waterfall taps, all very posh until you sat from this angle. The paintwork on the skirting boards was scratched and the ceiling could do with a clean. She spotted a little hole in corner, a mouse's, she wished she could join the mice, she would have felt safer all huddled together in between the walls. The shaking ebbed away as did the sweating and nausea. Tomorrow she would call her Psychiatrist that's for sure. She stayed by the loo not daring or wanting to move until morning . . .

The man walked past the police car, a young man and even younger woman sat in the car, bored. The man stooped towards the open window and held up a lead.

"Sir, you haven't seen a dog anywhere have you? Little bugger ran off, mixed breed, grey and small in height."

The police officer yawned. "Nah mate, maybe call the dog warden if you don't find him."

"Will do, he answers to the name of Ruin if you come by him, friendly little chap." And with that he marched off back in the direction of the park shouting "Ruin, come on boy."

PC Rachel White was brand new to the job, and eager. "Odd" she said, "the man said a small dog but he was really tall and had a tiny lead, like something you would have for a Mastiff" She looked at PC Tomlinson, he wasn't much more experienced than her, she supposed in some eyes still a rookie himself. She glanced at Tomlinson's long face, he hadn't been blessed with looks nor personality come to that.

"Fuck sake, what you on about? Just pass me some crisps and a coke and shut up yes?"

She did as he asked, he was never going anywhere in this job, but she had goals, one day she would be his boss and she would never let him forget being so cruel to her. She smiled a sarcastic smile.

As soon as he rounded the corner out of the view of the police car the artist jumped into his car. He was happy as the police guards or whatever you called them were always so young and naïve. So that's how much they valued Tess then, couldn't be bothered to get decent experienced cops to look out for her. That would make his pursuit much easier. He had staked out her trendy flat in the west end of Glasgow, it was too busy an area, too many people, too many tourist cameras and big brother everywhere. No he would think and plan the Grand Finale with attention to detail. Tess was worth that, she was the star of the show and the most perfect muse ever. He would hang around here for a while, get to know where she frequented, pubs where police hung out were a good place to just sit behind a book and listen, for alcohol loosens the tightest of tongues. He indicated and pulled his curvaceous jaguar out onto the road which was lined by cherry blossom trees.

Tess had prized herself from the toilet basin, jumped in the shower and got dressed in jeans, green pumps and a green string t-shirt, it was sweltering again so she scraped her hair away from her neck and face and stuck it in a low bun. Her body ached from the hard floor she had slept on, her breastbone had slightly bruised from lying over the pan and pain shot up her ass. She was exhausted, but needed to catch up with her psychiatrist as she had kept on putting it off. She poured black hot tea and took it just like that and wolfed down cornflakes with Oatley milk and fruit. She poured another tea as her phone rang.

"Hey Tess, it's Robyn are you ok to speak?"

This was never easy. "Ok as I will ever be" Tess replied.

"Right Tess, could you run me through what's been going on, on a scale of 1 to 10 your fear, anxiety and stress levels please and anything you could add." There was always a slight delay as the voice came through on her psychiatrist's line so she waited a few seconds before answering. She cleared her throat and gulped.

"I am at a 10. Nightmares, night sweats, terrors, vomiting, the shakes you know the usual. I keep going down the rabbit hole and opening doors, but its making things worse. I get the feeling some of this is memory but I am so confused. It's like I'm trying to remember but it's too traumatic." She held back on the emails she had received and also of her involvement with Patrick. "Oh and definitely remembered the day of my kidnap a guy came to deliver a parcel, asked if mum and dad were in as I was underage to sign for it, Jude my dog started growling a the man, so the guy just said he would come back later when my parents were home. I called mum and dad and they said they hadn't ordered anything?"

"Right ok let's deal with the stress levels first, we have a new therapy called tapping technique, I will send you a video of how to do it as its self-therapy, please keep on with it and if you don't get it call me and I will go through it. It's been very successful in trials we have conducted. The guy with the parcel is a little weird, he never came back or I suppose your parents would be out looking for you so could've missed him. Tess I would tell the police about this it could be important. Anything else that's happened in your life that could be triggering these attacks?"

Tess clearly heard Robyn sparking a fag on the other end of the phone; she liked this humanity that Robyn possessed. "I have shifted jobs and I'm working for a forensic archaeology unit out of Glasgow uni, we are investigating a murder, skeletal remains including a foetus have been unearthed. It's made me have flashbacks, but I was having them before this case?" Tess took a drink of her tea which was now cold, she spat it back into the cup. Tess felt the familiar exhaustion that came from talking to her therapist, she was mentally shattered but needed to get to work today. "Look I will do the tapping technique, thanks Robyn, I need to shoot as work beckons," she walked to the sink and refilled the kettle.

"Ok Tess, but please contact me if your triggers get any worse, and I know its easily said but you need to be careful you don't work yourself too hard, take care." The phone clicked off.

Tess called David as they would be working from her rented air B & B today, they were going to read papers on skeletal females with foetus burials, they needed to see if they could investigate, debate and theorise why this murder took place, was the foetus unknown to the murderer, or another victim, who was the woman they had excavated? Anything they could unearth could help the police catch this twisted killer. David arrived a half hour later. They discussed their theories about this burial, the disarticulation and the obvious knowledge the killer had about archaeology. Neither had ever heard or seen anything like this, it was copycat burying of ancient sites.

The Artist

He hung the painting on the wall alongside the others. She looked stunning. The detail he had painted of the blood running down his muse's neck was just genius, he had used some of her blood mixed with the paint and he thought that made the art exquisite. His muse had eventually known her fate, he had drugged her a little, he loved to watch them as their chests slowly stopped rising, he could almost feel their souls leaving their bodies. He couldn't believe it when she told him she was pregnant with twins, the gods would be very pleased, not only with his virility but also the double sacrifice of children, his children. However, the most exciting part of it all was when the flesh had fallen off the bones, he would then revisit the burial. Dig it back up so he could see the splendour of his work, and make his Grand Finale painting. The bitch, her sidekick and the cop had ruined that part for him and he was furious. He vowed revenge on them all, he would pray to his gods to help him achieve this.

Where Is My Daughter?

Tess had taken a shower and was deciding what to wear for this meal Patricks daughter Tess had organised. She had purchased a few new outfits as she was running low, she never expected to be dating. She didn't want formal or too much flesh on show, after all it was dinner with his daughter and maybe her boyfriend too. She eventually chose khaki green shorts but not too short, a blue and white striped tea shirt and brown espadrilles and matching bag. She brushed her hair to one side and wore a little make-up and topped it off with her favourite perfume. Gina had ordered her a cab to the restaurant whose food was supposed to be amazing. She arrived gave her name and was shown to a low table with cushions rather than seats in middle-eastern style, the cushions were different colours and all embellished with embroidery, tassels and jewels. It was stunning, the ceiling had been made to resemble a bell tents interior so went to a point then draped down dramatically, fairy lights had been dotted about, it was magical. Traditional Palestinian music played gently in the background. There were shishas dotted around their table, she had never tried one before, she would tonight. Patrick and Gina arrived together with no sign of her boyfriend. Tess was going to get up to greet them but Patrick put his hand out to indicate not to bother getting up.

"For fuck sake Gina, how the hell will we get up from the floor after a few drinks?" He tutted sat down next to Tess, leant over and kissed her cheek, she blushed.

"Dad, stop whining. With dad it's either a pub or curry, he's a stickler." Gina plonked herself down rather ungracefully on the opposite side of the table.

"Is you boyfriend not joining us Gina?" Tess asked.

Patrick punched the air and smiled mockingly.

"Dad! So rude. Sorry Tess he texted to say he was busy with work." She picked up a menu and beckoned for the waiter or waitress who seemed engrossed with each other. The waitress was young, pretty and looked of Pakistani heritage. She sashayed over then looked over her shoulder to make sure the waiter was watching her, and he was. Gina ordered red wine, Tess and Patrick ordered ice cold carafes of cold beer. The food sounded amazing, they ordered a mixed plater with meat and vegan options. The waiter brought their food over on large silver trays adorned with bright lace covers. On them were vine leaves stuffed with rice, the largest olives she thought she had ever seen, kebabs, hummus, falafels, some veg had been served on flaming hot plates which added to the atmosphere. The summer's heat gave you the impression you really were in the Palestine's. The more they chatted the more Tess bonded with Gina. She had great qualities and was fiercely loyal to her dad, which Tess admired.

"I don't suppose when Gina intruded the other day that she told you the full story about herself?" Patrick looked at Gina.

"Dad! Don't embarrass me," she rolled her eyes

"So Gina is a model, but she uses this to distract people from who she really is. She pretends to be dumb but that's an act, aye lassie?" Patrick picked up his beer and swigged it.

"Go on Gina, what are you hiding?" Tess asked inquisitively in between mouthfuls of glorious hummus and flat bread. Gina threw her dad a dirty look.

"I'm a microbiologist, I prefer modelling," she shrugged.

Tess held her beer towards Gina in a congratulations cheers motion, Gina clinked her glass on Tess's. They had such varied conversation and laughter that evening, Patrick and Gina were like a double act, they insulted each other, constantly punched one another's arms, hugged one another, it was a special connection and bond. He also kept calling her the hurricane which was a nickname that Tess understood why she had been given it. When they had finished up and paid for their meal Patrick said they should share a cab and drop Gina off at her boyfriends, she said it was fine she would text them when she arrived home, Tess was obviously staying the night with Patrick. Gina gave them both a hug then when her taxi arrived she headed out of the door with a backward glance and a wave. Tess and Patrick's taxi came not long after so they jumped in for the 10 minute journey back to his. As soon as they got over the threshold they practically tore each other's clothes off. Patrick's phone pinged he picked it up took a quick glance and read a text from Gina saying she had got to her boyfriend's safely. He texted her xxx back, then resumed where he had left off with Tess. He grabbed her hand and pulled her upstairs towards his bedroom. She couldn't get enough of his gym honed body and she knew the feeling was mutual. They landed on the bed with Patrick on top of her, it felt magical. They both came together, that was a first for Tess, she guessed not for Patrick. They fell asleep quickly as the beer and love making had drained their energy and both had work tomorrow. She had the most amazing sleep since she was 13. She felt safe with Patrick and had no nightmares.

They rushed breakfast which was just toast and tea as they had to stop off at Tess's to get her work things and for her to change, they had a good laugh in the car, everything felt very natural. She did a quick change and picked up her laptop and work case, David and her would be working in the lab today, putting the remaining parts of the skeleton back together for further study. Also, seeing if they could trace the girl through dental records. They decided to just take Patricks car, people were already gossiping and it didn't make sense taking 2 cars. When they arrived at the horrid ugly police station people stood gawping at them both, she heard a young police officer saying Patrick was a lucky sod. Patrick gave him a smile and wink. She would stay for the briefing and then join David at the lab. Patrick had held the box and its contents as evidence, they had sent the hair off for analysis, it might bring something up, but that hair was some girls DNA, or it might not be related to the victim at all, it could just be a wild goose chase, who knew. The briefing finished, Patrick bid farewell to Tess who blushed. Patrick's phone rang, he answered the call, spoke to a DNA expert, his expression changed quickly. He swiped to end the call.

"Tess," he shouted as he ran after her. "Wait".

Ben had left his phone at work last night which was annoying. He was snowed under as a business analyst and couldn't remember if Gina had said she was staying at his or her dads. He was relieved he had to work, her dad was a fucking nightmare and scary at that. He should've been a gangster never mind a cop, he was the most intimidating man Ben had ever come across, a scary Glaswegian Viking. He had a business breakfast to attend which went on for hours. He finally got hold of his phone around lunch time. He checked his messages. FUCK FUCK FUCK, he made a call.

The Artist

He was trying to recall the name of the US serial killer he had stolen this trick from. He had watched a documentary and thought it was clever, was it Bundy? Such a handsome man the same as himself, however that's where the similarity ended, I mean he wasn't a raving mad serial killer, he made offerings to appease his gods and also created amazing art. He had followed her cab from the restaurant it was so easy. As she got out of the cab, the artist alighted from his car quickly. He had a walking stick and a fake limp, he slipped and called for help.

Gina came rushing over."Hey, its ok I'll help you up," she said as she bent down to assist the poor man.

"Oh you are too kind, I think I better get back in my car and go home, I feel a little unsteady." He rose to his feet and wobbled. "Could you possibly get my glasses I think they have slid under my seat to the back, I would be awfully grateful." He smiled at her but the overhead light had been smashed so she couldn't see his face in any detail, she noticed she had crunched glass beneath her feet.

"Of course I will, bloody vandals honestly" She opened the back door and bent to try locate his glasses. She felt a thud across the back of her head, then blackness.

Tess came rushing back as Patrick shouted for her. He was about to say something when his phone went again. He looked at it angrily and not understanding why he would call.

"What?" Patrick ran his head through his hair in an anxious gesture.

"You fucking what" He screamed. "You were supposed to look after her, FUCK FUCK FUCK" He punched the wall. Tess had seen angry men but this was like he was a wild animal. She jumped as his punch landed. She moved forward concerned and rested her hand on his back. She thought he might rip out of his suit like the hulk.

"Fuck Tess, Gina didn't stay at Ben's last night, where's my baby?" he blew out air form his mouth.

"But the text?" Tess asked. "Let's call her first yeah?" Tess didn't even convince herself. Patrick called Gina's mobile, straight to answerphone, he called her agent. Gina hardly even wiped her arse without consulting her agent first. The agent picked up on the first ring.

"Hey, no, she's missed a job and a really good one at that, this is not like her," she said and she sounded pissed off.

Patrick didn't even answer her. "Tess grab everyone you can for an emergency meeting."

Patrick pulled out his phone again and bellowed at some poor sod. Everyone dashed to the meeting room, when Patrick said jump, people pole vaulted. He was furious at himself too, he was so concerned about Tess's safety he hadn't even thought his daughter might be in the firing line. Of course nothing was certain, but it was obvious that bastard had taken her, but who was the bastard, Tess's kidnapper was dead. He hadn't even told Tess about the hair yet, that's what he had called her back for. Tess was linked to the murder and burial of that poor girl and her babies, and his daughter being missing. They all gathered in the stifling meeting room, it doubled up as a board room but it was so shabby it was embarrassing. Off white paint peeled off the walls and the ancient radiators didn't work anymore. There was no air conditioning apart from in the cells. What a fucking joke that was, they had to acknowledge prisoners human rights but they had none. There weren't enough seats so those last stood at the back of the room. Some faces looked uncomfortable and Tess didn't think it was just from the stifling heat.

Patrick looked around the room and commanded attention.
"My fucking daughter has vanished and I want every man woman, dog or whatever on the case, you fucking hear me? I want my fucking daughter back alive and quickly!" The room seemed to shake as he shouted.

He pointed to Tess, "The locket of hair that was found in the burial has a DNA match in the system, it's Tess's hair, it's linked to Tess's abduction as a child, my daughter is with a fucking monster. I want you all on this, right now."

Tess's jaw nearly hit the floor, she was both horrified and irritated. How was that her hair? Patrick had no right telling people about her past, no right at all.

He pointed to two police officers. "You two get to her boyfriend's, go over everything with a fine toothcomb. Oh and bring him in with you when you come back." He barked out more orders and people dispersed as though someone had thrown a grenade.

A rookie policewoman came towards Patrick but her partner pulled her back, and said something angrily in her ear.

"You," Patrick pointed at her. "You, what were you going to say?"

She looked a little nervous but walked towards Patrick.

"Well sir, sorry sir I am just a rookie. Not sure if this means anything?" Tess recognised her as half of the partners who had been tailing or protecting her, whichever way you viewed it. Tess walked forward too. The rookie nodded to Tess.

"Well, we were watching the Docks and a man came past looking for a dog." She looked embarrassed.

"What?" Patrick shook his head in disbelief. "And," he prompted impatiently.

"Well, I said to my colleague it was weird, that the man had a tiny lead but he was very tall, he said his lost dog was small. I found it odd that he would have to stoop over to walk his dog so relayed this to my colleague who said I was talking rubbish. Anyhow, I saw the man again when I was going to the book shop and he was coming out." She really felt stupid now this was wasting time. Her career was over before it began.

"Which book shop?" Patrick asked

"The one on Albion Street, on the corner."

Tess interrupted the conversation. "Ok can you remember any details about him?" she liked this girl.

"Nothing much. I recall he got into an old car and he had a book under his arm, but I didn't get a registration. I was in a rush."

Tess grabbed hold of her hand. "Think, please, anything at all." She still had a tight grip of the rookie's hand.

"Yes, the book had a picture of standing stones or something? I'm sorry." She smiled apologetically. Tess looked at Patrick astounded.

Patrick grabbed the rookie and kissed the top of her head. "I want you to go with PC Moran and the sketch artist. I want every single thing you can remember. You're fucking promoted."

He nodded to Tess. "Come with me," but dragged her off before the words were out of his mouth. Tess half ran and followed him to his car.

"Let me drive," she held her hands out for the keys.

"No." he knocked her hand away.

"Now," she said as she grappled his keys from his hand.

He didn't have time to argue, God knows how much time his precious daughter had. They jumped in with Tess in the driving seat. Tess floored the car, she took bends like she raced for Maclaren's. Patrick's knuckles turned white trying to grip anywhere he could. He looked at her in astonishment.

"My dad was into rallying, so was I." That's all she said, another story for another time, hopefully. They got to the book shop in 10 minutes, it should take 25. They pulled up outside the shop and parked on double yellow lines. No time to abide the law. The book shop was in an old stone building, it was pretty and inviting, it had windows that had small glass panes with their frames painted a sage green. A canvass type awning hung over the windows, written in gold was Needful things, very clever thought Tess, you name a bookshop after a book written by the greatest horror author ever, Stephen King. As they entered a bell chimed, how twee she thought, on a different occasion this would be a great place to stop by. Patrick practically ran to the counter. A woman of about 18 years old stood behind it. She had bright red hair, a ring through her nose and tattoos on her neck. Trying not to be judgmental but being judgemental Tess thought she would be useless for information, if it were her working that day. Tess scanned the room, the bookshelves were crammed full. It really was a beautiful shop. The girl didn't look up from the book she was reading. Patrick grabbed it out of her hand.

"Hey," she objected, showing her tongue piercing now. "What the hell?"

Patrick pulled out his police ID, the girl put her hands up like he had pulled out a gun. "Were you working on the 14th of July? If not who was?" he handed the book back to her.

"I'm here 6 days a week, mum and dad are fucking slave drivers, why what's up?" She picked at black nail polish on her stubby fingernails. Patrick clicked his fingers in front of her face.

"Attention," he almost shouted, but it worked, he had scared the girl into an almost hypnotic gaze. "There was a man came in that day, bought an archaeology book, do you remember him." Tess smiled at the girl, she felt sorry for her.

"I can do better than that," she replied. "Mum and dad insist the camera is on as I'm on my own in the shop. We never erase the tapes; we have like year's worth of them. Here I'll show you." She beckoned for them to follow her through a door round the back of the counter. Tess's phone rang, caller ID said it was David, shit she forgot to call him and let him know what was going on.

"Tess, are you OK?" he asked. She quickly told him the story and heard him gasp.

"Tess, we have the bones of 3 different girls here, not one," he exhaled sharply.

"Shit, so serial killer?" Patrick turned round abruptly and shot Tess a look. She handed him the phone, "you need to hear this."

She didn't think she had ever seen anyone turn as white as Patrick just did. Patrick didn't say bye to David, he wasn't ordinarily a man of pleasantries and certainly not today.

"Carry on," he ordered the girl.

She went through the tapes until she found what she was looking for, popped it into the archaic video player and they crowded round to watch. A man entered the shop; he looked in some ways regal. He spoke with the girl, Andy her name was, and you could see her directing him to the archaeological and history department. At the moment all you could really see was the top of his head.

"It gets better," the girl picked up on what they were thinking. "We have another camera that takes over different angle." As she said that the man came into view completely. He was 50 or maybe a little older, distinguished and somewhat regal looking, he held himself well but also a little arrogantly. He spoke with an Eton educated English drawl, if you listened closely though you would hear a bit of a Scottish accent, albeit a very posh one. Like a lord or someone who had been educated in England at the finest school. Tess was deep in thought.

"Tess," Patrick shouted at her now, she jumped.

"Yes?" For fuck sake she nearly said Sir. "Tess, look at the book he's chosen." Tess watched the screen, she felt dizzy and sick. It was a book she had written herself titled "The Art of an Archaeological Burial". She gasped.

"Who the fuck is he Tess? Who the fuck has my girl" The girl, Andy, looked at Tess confused. Tess could feel herself slipping down the Rabbit hole.

"Patrick I have no idea who that is, I'm sorry." Patrick pulled out his phone again and called the station. He spoke to the desk sergeant. He was older than Patrick, late 40s, he looked older though. His hair had receded and turned grey. He had a bulbous nose with red veins from his love of Whisky, but he was a good man.

"Yes. It's me. I want that girl rookie on my daughter's case here right away if she has finished her statement. Take her off whatever she is doing she has an excellent nose." He spoke in a softer manner to the sergeant as he had known him years, they liked a pint together and shared a love for whisky.

"Listen mate, anything at all I can do? I am staying late tonight and overnight if need be to help ok, we will find her. You take care mate," He replied in a sombre note. He had known Gina since she was 8, she was like his granddaughter. When Patrick rung off, sarge as he was known wiped tears from his eyes and cleared his throat.

Gina

Something wasn't right. Gina went to feel the back of her head as it pounded. She was sure she hadn't carried on drinking when she had got to Bens last night as today she had such an important modelling assignment. She tried to open her eyes but she felt like she was wading through thick fog. What the fuck? Her hand couldn't reach her head as something was restricting her movement. She gingerly lifted her head off where ever it lay and she felt it sticking to what felt like a pillow. Blood! She was sure of it. Finally her eyes opened but still blurry, she kept on widening them to help focus. She blinked then finally she could see. Her hands were shackled to an old metal bed frame as were her ankles. She was confused and started to panic. She lifted her knees one at a time in like a running motion at the same time she looked up. What the Fuck? Sheer terror took over, she began to weep, and hyperventilate. The ceiling was made up of bones, thousands of what she thought were human bones! From the centre hung the most macabre monstrosity she had ever seen. A chandelier made from human skulls and bones, it took centre place demanding you look at it.

"Daddy, oh Daddy," she sobbed. She had never had a mother to call out to, just her gran and her dad, her gran was now gone, it was just her and dad. As her memory started to come back she chastised herself for being so stupid and off-guard, and her a fucking police chiefs daughter.

"Welcome back," The Artist said in his posh drawl, he elongated his words so back became baaack, hello became hellllooooo and so forth. He had plans for the wretched police chief's daughter, big plans he better get to work.

The Rookie

She had to kick herself. I mean the circumstances were horrific but still. Her police work had paid off and gave them their first real lead. PC Rachel White (the rookie) had been told that she would be fast tracked through her training, then straight to detective. She was only 19. She finished off her statement then went to meet Patrick, she meant chief. He had some tapes for her to go through. She walked down the long corridor towards the room where they examined CCTV, it was grey and dull like everything in this station. She felt like she was on death row in some ways, a little trepidation kicking in now. If she blew this her name would be shit, it's a long way up but a quick slide down. She stopped to check her hair was in place before knocking.

"Come in," Patrick bellowed. She went for the door handle, stopped and squeezed her fist for a few seconds then went to open the door. Patrick opened it from his side at the same moment and she almost fell flat on her face.

"Look, I don't have time for fucking formalities every single second counts. I want you to go through the CCTV. I want you to take note of anything about that sick twat, anything. Cancel any plans you have as we are working round the clock until my daughter is home, yes?"

He put his hand on her shoulder gave it a slight squeeze and a very slight nod of his head. She would do her best. She vaguely knew Gina. When Gina was in England they would go to the same schools, although Gina was 3 years her senior. It was a bit weird, Gina's childhood was all over the place, sometimes Glasgow and sometimes here. If Patrick did have time to pick Gina up from school you would see the teachers, mothers and teenage girls swooning, for he was so young and fit. She felt her cheeks blush and started trawling through the CCTV.

Tess

Tess had got a cab to the laboratory as obviously Patricks day had turned out like a horror film. She slung her bag over her shoulder and entered the lab. She rushed towards David.

"David, oh God." David put his arms out and gave her a big hug. She had never felt like not working so much in her life, but Gina's life could depend on it. She also knew she had to get into her own mind, for it held the answers. She and David gathered round the skeleton, they now had 3 different numbers as three different people. They pulled out 2 more examination tables. Each skeletal remains would now have their own table and hopefully story. They wore gloves and handled the bones gingerly. The pelvis bone was on its own as David had identified it as having a different owner to the other bones. Question was which skeleton if any the foetuses belonged to? So they examined the pelvic bone with a fine tooth comb. They noticed a series of shotgun pellet like pockmarks on the inside of the bone. Whoever this woman had been had given birth at some point, but it didn't tell them anything more about the foetuses, so they could belong to Bone 1 as they had labelled her. They also knew that they wouldn't know from the pockmarks how many children she had had. They took numerous photos and also inputted this information into a recording chart on their laptops. They moved along to the remains labelled 2. Teeth and 2 rib bones. Tess looked perplexed. David explained to Tess what he had discovered while she wasn't here.

"So," he whistled, "these teeth don't belong to that skull." He waited for it to sink in.

"What?" mouthed Tess.

"The poor victim had her teeth extracted, hopefully post-mortem. Then the perpetrator glued someone else's teeth in their place." he glanced at Tess sideways and put his hands up in a shrug.

"Ok, Ok, so teeth and 2 rib bones?" She took a sip of her bottled water. "So where are the rest of them?" Something came to her mind about teeth, but it left her before she had time to grab the thought, she made a note in her journal, so she could think at some point. They went on to the skeleton labelled 3, a skull minus teeth, a pelvis and 2 rib bones?

"So Tess, it gets even more interesting. I had chance to radiocarbon date the bones. 3 is very recent and modern. 1 is 600-700 hundred years old. 2 is 10-30 years."

Tess's eyebrows shot up. "So we have serial killer who's a vampire, what the fuck David?" She let out a nervous laugh. This just got crazier and crazier.

"Oh," he hadn't finished yet. "The artefact, deer bones are roughly 2-5 years old, they have butcher's marks on them, too." He went to the phone and asked the receptionist to order 2 coffees and sandwiches, he was starving and he thought Tess might be too.

When she had regressed down the rabbit hole why did she see a deer, one with missing ribs? The Deer had paused as though to tell her something. She called her Psychiatrist as they took break. Her Psychiatrist or therapist whichever or however you wanted to view it answered promptly.

"Hey Robyn it's me," said Tess as she cradled her phone between her ear and shoulder, while she wrote some notes.

"Hey Tess, what's up?" Tess liked Robyn's casual tone, it almost felt she was confiding in a friend.

"Robyn, I want regression therapy, like now?" David handed her a strong black coffee and held up a sandwich like it was a football trophy. She didn't mind David overhearing her conversation, she felt comfortable with him too and had divulged her past.

"Mmmm, ok, why?" Robyn sounded apprehensive.

"I have to go back to my past, someone's life is at stake. It's the only way to save her." Tess thought how much Patrick must be hurting and she knew he partially blamed her.

Robyn let out a sigh, "Ok as your therapist I would advise against it as you are my priority and patient. Tess, it can have terrible consequences forcing memories. Your brain suppresses them for a reason, it is to protect you from harm. So maybe you will save this person but you could be sacrificing your own sanity and possibly life." Tess could hear the concern in Robyn's voice, she knew the possible implications and danger.

"Ok, I will take that risk. Please arrange it for me for this evening, I'll pay privately." Robyn agreed albeit not enthusiastic at all. She told Tess she would find her a local specialist and try to arrange it ASAP. As they ended their conversation Tess phone went again. It was Patrick.

"Tess, you need to think or regress or whatever to help Gina, I can't fucking stand this its torture," his voice wavered with emotion.

Tess was a little perturbed. "Patrick, this isn't easy at all, I have trauma that has never been dealt with that you can't even comprehend going through. I'm trying I really am!' She just swiped the red icon to end the call, she didn't need the pressure, it didn't help her remember.

Tess 2007

Her kidnapper kept on coming back into that dark place. She would hear him on the phone again, talking to someone telling them lies. She had never really thought about that before, that her kidnapper had been talking about her to someone on the outside. The bunker, that's what she decided to call it, that's the only thing she could think it might be, she had recently studied about the Second World War so knew people had built bunkers to shelter. The constant sound of dripping water filled her senses again, she thought she would go mad. It's weird when you have so much time to think, your brain still needs something to focus on.

At first you just think fight or flight, then realise there will be neither, you kind of accept your fate in a way, turn your brain off of fight or flight and focus on other things. At first she had focused on the concrete floor, then the brick walls. She had counted the bricks she could see 454 bricks in total. It was then that she had noticed a broken tile. She stretched her leg as far as she could, using her toes as fingers she tried to grab the tile, it was exhausting. It took her 5 days and she thought a few hours to get to the tile. If only you could understand her achievement. When you see underdog athletes win a race or football, that's how she felt, she felt exhilarated and hungry. Her left foot was scratched and cut from the effort, if it was painful but she failed to feel it. Oh, she had felt pain during her time here, a bit of sore foot wouldn't bother her.

She heard her captor come down the stairs so she hid the piece of tile under a pipe behind her, her handcuffs would reach just far enough. She glared at him. He strode over to her and was an imposing sight. She didn't recoil now, wouldn't let him have the satisfaction. "Small victories" her dad would say when she started to stand up to the school bully. Then he would kiss the top of her head, how protected she had felt.

"I need food," she demanded. She looked up and challenged him. He had a potted beef sandwich and threw it in her lap.

"I don't eat meat." That wasn't entirely true. However, from this day forward, if she survived she would never eat meat again for she knew how it felt to be caged, beaten, your life hanging in someone else's hands.

"Fucking eat it, bitch," he roared and loomed over her now. She took a huge bite, chewed it then spat it in his face. He had bits of chewed up beef and bread, mixed with saliva hanging from his face and clothes. He drew his hand back and punched her in the face. Her head snapped back so hard she thought her neck had broken. Fucking moronic fool. She laughed at him. He looked confused. The arsehole had so much of her DNA on him, if he killed her he would be caught, eventually. He finished . . . well use your imagination, Tess refused to think about what he did on numerous occasions. He left abruptly, Tess felt for the piece of tile, she found it and felt relieved.

Tess 2022

"Patrick, I, I can't, I'm sorry," she swiped her phone and cut him off. Although she felt his pain she couldn't, wouldn't tolerate abuse, besides she couldn't remember. She got confused. Her dog Jude had survived his injuries but that's most of what she knew. It meant she didn't have to venture down the rabbit hole. She knew though that her journey down there would have to begin this evening, when the expert in regression took her there. She breathed in deeply then exhaled loudly.

The Artist

He had locked his captive in the cellar. She wasn't really refined enough to be in the grand bone room. She was just a pawn really. He would toy with her like a cat with a mouse, after all that was part of the game, his game and he made the rules. Her dad would be out of his mind with worry. Well that's tough; the artist wanted Tess, his Tess. Patrick had tainted his beautiful muse, just like the captor he had entrusted her with all those years ago. How dare anyone touch her? She was to be given to the gods. First he would paint her in all her beauty, his muse. Then he would start thinking about the offerings that would go with her to the other side, this was very important, get it wrong and he would anger his gods. He had already angered them all those years ago, his failure had been excruciating. He unlocked the drawer of an antique chest, French, the ornate carvings were mesmerising. He pulled out a phone, very basic. They wouldn't be able to trace it. He would use it once anyhow, and then get rid of it. He had Patrick's number, he was clever. He dialled and waited for an answer. Patrick picked up straight away.

"Who is this?" he bellowed down the phone.

Gosh he was rude wasn't he? "Oh Patrick, be polite now. After all I have your daughter, she is exquisite," he chuckled down the phone. Patrick had only ever felt faint once before, that's when he had broken his leg during rugby. It wasn't the pain but the sight of the bloody bone protruding from his skin, the fibula? Tess would know which one. He felt a moment of regret but didn't have time to dwell on it.

Patrick's hands were sweating, the phone felt like it was going to fall any moment now, so did Patrick. "I want my baby, alive! You hear me? I want my fucking baby girl!" He felt a tear sting his face, he seldom cried, the last time when he lost Nan a few months back. God he wished she was here now. Are you sometimes on the phone and you can almost feel someone's reaction? Patrick pretty much felt the Artist's superiority and the mocking.

"Oh, now, now Patrick. You are in no position to order me about. At any time I can slit your pretty daughter's throat open wide and feed her to the pigs, or worse use, your imagination she is a very attractive girl. Patrick, Patrick calm down, I can just imagine your face. It's a hoot," he sniggered into the phone.

Patrick ran his hands through his hair. He inhaled deeply, he had to remain professional. How would he react in this situation if it wasn't his daughter?

"I'm listening," Patrick replied. He had a pen in his hand and was drawing a hangman. He was going to kill this fucker. The call would be put on trace, but no one these days was that stupid.

'Patrick, I am going to make you an offer you can't refuse, well you could but then I will kill your daughter. Your daughter isn't really my type you see, so I want an exchange, Tess for your girl and don't even think about using a cop as exchange, I have been watching Tess all these years so I know her. I will give you 24 hours to sleep on it and I fully expect a decision tomorrow at 4pm, no later."

All Patrick could hear after that was a dial tone, it reminded him of a person flatlining on a hospital machine, death, that's all he could hear, death. He picked up the phone and called Tess.

Gina

Gina had decided to change tack, she needed to dig deep and find the courage of a lioness. After all she was Patrick's daughter, all feisty and mouthy. Nothing like her weak mother who lost herself to heroin. In fact her mother had given her up at birth. Patrick was just 14 and her mother 19. She had been his babysitter a few years back so her pregnancy had caused a massive scandal, what with him being underage too. Her mother was just a vessel, in fact after giving birth her mother left the hospital and spiralled into heroin addiction. She died from an overdose when Gina was just 2. It was Patrick's Nan who had gone to the hospital and fought tooth and nail with the authorities for Gina. Patrick as a minor really had no say and was too young to get his own place or a job. Yet Patrick was there right from the beginning, he idolised his daughter. They settled in Glasgow for a while until Patrick finished school, then when he was 18 he applied for the police and got in. His nan would take on the responsibility of most of Gina's care. However Patrick never shirked his duty as a father and would take over as soon as his shift finished. It was exhausting but worth everything to both he and Nan. So she wouldn't allow herself to be weak like her mother, not ever, she wasn't going to die without a fight.

She needed to understand her captor on some level. She had to let go of the terror in which her surroundings bore down like quicksand pulling you under. She opened her eyes and took it all in. He had decided to move her from the cellar, he said he wanted to share something with her. The grandiose nature of the bones and ceiling was when you got over the shock were pretty spectacular. This couldn't only be only her captor's work as he would've needed to kill about 100 people a day to achieve this over a long period of time. This had to be historic and symbolic. The person who would be able to answer these questions was Tess, how ironic.

The Artist

He knew there was no way Patrick would let Tess come to him. Not because he loved Tess more than his daughter, because he was a police officer and that simply wouldn't be allowed. They would in fact send a double, even though he had told them he would be able to tell. The point was, they were stupid imbeciles who would fall into his trap. That was the problem with the lower classes, they just weren't as bright as the well-bred upper classes. Why did people think we have an issue in politics when people who could barely speak the queens English were put into power? At least the conservatives were mostly old Etonians. He opened unlocked the door to where Gina was held, his favourite place on earth.

Tess 2022

Earlier she had attempted the tapping therapy technique that Robyn had coached her through, it had made her violently sick. She now turned her phone off as instructed by the regression therapist. Robyn had got her an immediate appointment. She felt nervous. Ainsley the therapist was about 35, pretty with gorgeous afro hair, her skin the colour of mocha, but her eyes were a startling green, she could almost transfix you with her gaze. Tess lay on the therapy table, she looked around her at the beautiful paintings of nature, mountains, beaches, Lochs and glens. The walls were painted a soft off white, nothing in here would dazzle you apart from Ainsley's eyes. Ainsley smiled then spoke with a soft Northern accent, Yorkshire Tess thought.

"So Tess, you know this comes with its dangers? I could open a door that should remain closed in your head. That's why our minds work as they do, to protect us from trauma we just can't deal with or process."

Tess nodded, she didn't really want to speak as her voice didn't really match with the nod she had given in consent, she was petrified.

"Ok, I need you to take very deep breaths and relax. I want you to focus your mind on a white sandy beach, focus on the way the sand feels between your toes, the way the ocean feels when it laps up against you. Can you feel it Tess?" Tess nodded gently.

"These feelings remind you of the last time you felt safe, really safe, Tess. Can you tell me about a time like this?" Ainsley dimmed the lights more with a remote control.

Tess could almost feel herself floating, she felt at ease at peace. That feeling you get as a child when you are sandwiched in between both parents in bed. That sense of safety. There was nothing like it.

"I was young, very young. In bed between mum and dad, I felt so warm and secure. Dad was laughing and complaining I was a fidget. Fidget fidget should've called you Bridgette, and mum was laughing too."

Ainsley was slightly confused. It suggested that Tess would've been about what maybe 5 when she had that memory. Ainsley had thought Tess would've brought up a more recent memory, just before her kidnap.

"That's an awful long time ago Tess. Are there no newer safe memories than that?"

Tess twitched her legs anxiously. Her breathing became rapid

"Tess, I want you to remain calm, ok? Nothing can happen to you now. I want you to regress but without the dread and fear. I want you to feel the ocean lapping against you and the sand between your toes ok?" Ainsley brought over a chair and adjusted it so she was level with Tess.

"This was the last time I felt truly safe, that's the morning, before you know, it happened."

Ainsley picked up her notes, fearful she had got Tess confused with another client. She re-read them. No, Tess was definitely kidnapped aged 13, so realistically she should be regressing to just before that incident.

"Ok Tess, very calmly, I want you to tell me why you don't feel safe after that morning snuggling with your parents. How old were you?"

Ainsley could see Tess's eyes moving rapidly under her lids.

"I was 6, in primary school. It feels wrong and I don't like it, I feel ashamed."

"What happened in primary Tess? You mustn't feel ashamed. Just let the truth flow." Ainsley took a gulp of water.

"The man, I don't like him. He strokes my hair but his hands are clammy and damp, his breath smells of strong coffee."

"Think carefully Tess, who is he, why is he in your school?"

'He's a historian I think? He takes an interest in me, leads me away, asks me why I like history. I am too young to know the difference really between history and archaeology. I tell him I love Stonehenge and the ring of Brodgar, he strokes my hair again and calls me something, Mose, Mouse. No he calls me his Muse his perfect Muse. He leads me to the caretaker's cupboard, a man with him nods and stands watching to make sure no one sees. I, I it's dark and I'm scared, I want my dad, I call for daddy. He puts one hand over my mouth, the other in my pants and it hurts, so, so much. When he is done he stands up and says something. I don't want to remember," Tess shakes her head from side to side as if she could banish the thought from her mind. "When he leaves I just stand there and pee my pants, I am so ashamed."

Ainsley didn't expect to hear this. Tess must've put this so far to the back of her mind, poor, poor child. She pushed one last time but for now she wouldn't, couldn't put Tess through anymore.

"Tess, I need to know who he was and why he was there. You said he wasn't there as a historian so what then?"

"He was an important politician's brother, a local conservative MP."

Ainsley brought Tess into the present and Tess threw up all over the floor.

The Rookie

The Rookie called Patrick's phone and he answered with a snap. "Yes?"

"Sir, sorry to bother you sir."

"Fucking Jesus, just get on with it, never mind apologising. Time is of the essence here."

"Sorry, Sir," she repeated and grimaced at her mistake but continued, "I've been going through the CCTV and I know that the man's face from somewhere, I just can't put my finger on it." She grimaced again ready for a bollocking.

"Think, Ok think, you have a good brain and eye for detail which is more than most. I want you to really concentrate. Go back through the CCTV until it clicks into place and it will." He said goodbye as he didn't want to alienate the only positive cop he had at his dispense.

She went back through the CCTV, she would go through it until something jogged her memory. Mostly she wanted to get Gina home and the kidnapper behind bars. Although a rookie, she could see that Patrick was a good man and a fair boss. Not one for small talk or pleasantries, however you knew where you stood with him, he didn't have a smokescreen he was hiding behind. She also wanted to prove to people she had what it takes and a good inquisitive brain. She had hated school, was told she wouldn't amount to much and basically bunked off smoking. Aged 18 she really got into the gym and took a police physical test on the gym equipment, realised she was fit enough and applied. The rest is history. Her phone pinged, it was her dad.

Hey bestest ever daughter x
Are you home in time for Question Hour? Xxx
If not I will save it and we can watch it together at some point x

Question Hour was a political debating programme they had always watched with each other. She was a bit geeky that way.
Hey super-dad ☺
Please save it and as soon as I am off I will buy wine and a take-away for us
Love U xxx
Ok Sweety xxx

She swiped the screen of her phone to turn it to vibrate only, stood up to get a coffee, then plonked herself hard back in the chair.
She ran her hands through her hair, a startled look on her face, she was about to call Patrick when he barged into the stuffy little room.

The Politician And His Secret Brother

He called his secretary who answered at once. "Let the house know I have the dreaded covid, feel awful so will have to isolate. Put me through to the prime minister at once." No airs or graces, no thank you. God, the secretary despised this man. She called the prime minister office and put him through.

The politician was in his private wing of the family's castle. It was completely separate from the downstairs where The Artist, his brother would come to life. Staff knew only to disturb him if he requested. Staff were just shit on his very expensive Italian shoes. He curtly answered the maids knock.

"Enter." She put down a tray of the finest tea in bone china and cucumber sandwiches. He shooed her away with his hand. Like you would a fly from your food. He cradled the phone under his chin until the PM came on the line.

"Now then good chap, how are we on this fine summer evening?" The politician held the PM in contempt too, for really he should've got the job. However he put on his finest voice.

"Oh my great friend and old Etonian, how the devil are you? I hear you have the dreaded lurgy old chap." The PM sat back and inhaled deeply on his cigar.

'Yes, oh yes, this appalling covid thing has wiped me out somewhat. It's all this mixing with the working classes, they're dirty my old boy. That will be me out for 10 days now old boy, just thought I would keep you in the loop," wha wha wha he laughed, nasally and haughtily.

Wha wha wha, the PM laughed too, like some moronic hyena, like most privileged aristocrats.

"Maybe we should open the mines back up, old boy and keep them down there, just throw them scraps from our enormous table, wha wha wha."

The Politician picked at his cucumber sandwich unaware that his maid had spat in it. He chewed impatiently.

"Oh, you do make me laugh old chap. I will see you in the private men's club once you're well, we will have caviar and champagne. For now old chap, take care."

"Likewise," replied The Politician. He put down the phone, and then summoned his maid to make more sandwiches.

"Of course sir, anything you wish." She put down the phone and smirked.

He picked up his pay as you go mobile phone, he had also had it scrambled to be on the safe side. He had just told a techy guy at MI5 he was having an affair with a married woman and needed security. The techy was fairly new and very ambitious, so did as he was asked. The Politician had hid his brother the artist's existence for most of their lives, occasionally though he needed to get involved to save his brother, his brother had a sickness worse than his own. He dialled Patrick's number as it was nearing 4 o'clock. This clever little device would also hide his accent. Patrick answered immediately.

"Yes?" he clicked his fingers so surveillance listened in.

"I presume you will be ready for our exchange? And that's not a question Patrick it's an order! At 22:00 hours tomorrow evening you will bring Tess to Edinburgh, to Arthur's Seat. I will be watching you closely. I will bring your daughter if you co-operate. Do you understand?" He smiled broadly, not only did he love the power, but the thought of getting the exquisite Tess back to his brother made him aroused. Oh, the power he yielded, he was superior to most, he had been chosen through a long heritage lineage, almost a god, well they would be once his brother had offered the perfect Tess to his gods with all her grave goods and offerings. You see they had an amazingly rich life as a mere mortals and were keen that it would continue on the other side too. They wanted to take that power and superiority into the spirit world when their time came.

"Edinburgh?" Patrick replied and was uncomfortable with this switch of countries. It's not how he had imagined it in his head.

"Edinburgh," replied The Artist and cut the phone off. Once Tess was back here he would head back down to his constituency in Leeds, leave Tess to her fate with his brother. He had made a mistake years earlier when his brother had arranged for the first kidnap, he felt his brother had been foolish to bring the child to the castle, even though she was drugged it seemed too risky. He had insisted his brothers trusted employee that thug would take her back to Leeds, leave her in the boot of a car that would never be traced, they had hope she would suffocate in the boot on that hot summers day, but she had come round alerting a passerby to her whereabouts. Damn her, damn her to hell.

Patrick stood there, that uncomfortable flatline sound again. He had an ominous feeling and he didn't like it. He called Tess again. She picked up and sounded drained.

He asked about the regression therapy. She told him everything and how the therapist would not put her through anymore in that sitting. Patrick felt like someone had hit him in the stomach, he tried not to wretch. The thought of some inhuman vile shit touching a childlike that disgusted him. He immediately thought of Gina at that age, he punched the wall, tried to regain his composure. He then told Tess about the exchange demand. She inhaled sharply.

"I will do it, anything to get Gina." Sweat poured from her yet she felt like ice had been injected into her veins. She took a strong black coffee from the lab vending machine, it tasted like she felt, rotten.

"That is not an option, Tess, and even if it was it's not something I would ask of you, it would end up with you both dead. I want you and David to work in the lab all night if you have to, to try get somewhere with this. It's all about you Tess so I think we will find the answer somewhere. I am going to get an officer to convey to your parents what you just told me, if that's ok? They might have something anything we can work with." He rubbed his temples fatigued.

'Ok, but I never told mum and dad and have obviously blocked it from my mind, I will have more regression therapy in the morning fingers crossed," she said. She took another gulp of the vile hot black liquid, she glanced at the bottom of the plastic cup, the coffee was dark and gloopy it looked like a muddy river bed, she was wading through mud and walking into the abyss.

"Tess, I love you'."

She was astounded and about to say the same but he ended the call.

Patrick marched over to the CCTV room where the rookie was working and put Tess's parent's number in front of her.

"Call them, ask what school, what year then trace back, I want to know in particular from the school the name of a historian who was also a politician who gave a talk to primary kids. I want to know if Tess changed in any way around that time?" He was about to leave when the rookie grabbed his arm.

"Sir, did you say politician? Something somewhere resonates." She flicked her long dark hair from her face and looked at him seriously. He took her shoulders gingerly, pleading with her to place her thoughts.

"Think. " He nodded to her then left.

She thought hard, why would she be thinking of a politician? She stood and stretched her limbs and rolled her neck. The room was stifling hot. She needed air and cold water from the machine. She went down the dull corridor, placed a pound coin in the vendor, a perfectly chilled bottle of water rolled out of the bottom drawer. She took the water unscrewed the lid and took large gulps, she then opened the door and got some air. The evening air smelled of grass and flowers, though she didn't know why as the station sat in an ugly concrete jungle. Crickets chirped and birds sang their last song of the evening. The wafting aroma of the Indian take-away nearby made her stomach gurgle. She had cleared her head so went back down the dull corridor into the CCTV room. She looked at the images of the man in the bookshop and recalled details of his face from when he had stopped by the police car looking for his imaginary dog. She had an idea. She switched on another screen and it whirred lazily in protest at been woken from cyber sleep. She brought up images of the House of Commons. She looked at archived news feeds of the house. These were often shown on a loop, the debates often tedious, members would often be sleeping which annoyed the fuck out of her, they got paid to attend. When she found the links she wanted to watch she picked up the phone and dialled the number Patrick had given her. Tess's dad answered and was alarmed when she said it was the police. She got the school and year that Tess would've attended aged 6, although there was nothing she could really do at this time of night regarding the school. She would contact St Mary's primary, in the Headingley area of Leeds first thing. For now she would work through the night examining the House of Commons. PC Tomlinson put his head round the door.

"Hey, how's my little lackey doing huh? Doing shit jobs for Patrick no doubt." He smiled that god awful smile. He looked even uglier with just the glare of computer screens lighting up his face, like something from a funfair ghost walk.

"Yep, you got that right, just doing shit rookie jobs. What do you want?" She glanced up at him.

"Well, cos I'm a good guy and we are here all night I'm taking orders for the Indian take-out. Want anything?" he asked.

"Make mine a veggie Madras with Chapatti please." She dug in her handbag found her purse and gave him a tenner. His hand lingered on hers as she passed him the note. He made a gesture with his crotch, "Oh veggie? Maybe you need some meat, maybe that's why you're so tense." With that he laughed and left her alone.

What a misogynistic twat, she thought. When he returned later with her food she beckoned him over suggestively with her index finger. He smiled and went over to her eagerly. She grabbed his crotch, twisted and dug in her nails. "That's your last warning mate."

Patrick appeared in the doorway.

"You are absolutely correct that's his last warning. Now get the fuck out of my station you're suspended until this investigation has been completed." PC Tomlinson went as white as a sheet, made no attempt to argue and left quickly. Patrick nodded at the Rookie, she smiled back.

"Anything from Tess's parents?"

'Yes, so obviously they clarified school year, etc. Her dad was devastated though and I heard her mum cry out in the background. Her dad said around that time she did become more introverted, they never suspected anything as he said she was always a studious child. He said she just studied more, but did wet the bed for a few years after. They are getting a plane from Corfu to Glasgow as soon as possible. I will call the school as soon as they open, though I doubt they have records or even the same staff from that long ago."

"Good work, good work, keep it up," he nodded again and left. He needed to work out how they would trap the kidnapper, his daughter's life depended on it. He called Mike who was the head of surveillance and they arranged a meeting in 20 minutes. He grabbed a tea on the way as he had to keep awake and alert, then headed to the board room. Mike was not what people expected. He was really nondescript. Unlike the movies real-life surveillance and undercover work required agents to be unremarkable. In the movies it was always people you would remember, good looking and impressive.

Agents like Mike relied on people not noticing them; you would walk past them in a park without as much as a glance. He had no distinct features, nose not big or small, no scars on his face or tattoos, he did wear glasses although didn't need them.

Mike stood up from his chair and shook Patrick's hand and put his other hand over Patricks and squeezed in a comforting gesture. The board room was one of the better rooms in this concrete shit hole. It had to be as Patrick and his colleagues would sometimes meet the mayor and politicians in this room. The walls were painted with expensive paint in contrast to the cheap peeling paint of interrogation rooms. A picture of the queen hung from the wall, watching them intently, it seemed that her eyes followed you, it was creepy. It would be replaced by a picture of the King later on that year. There were paintings of London, Edinburgh and Cardiff as though other cities didn't matter, realistically they didn't. The police budgets in smaller cities were nothing like the budgets of the capitals and it often showed statistically.

"Lies, damned lies, and statistics."

One of Patrick's favourite quotes. His suit jacket felt tight around his biceps, he took it off and threw it over the chair. Mike poured them both some water, then cleared his throat.

"We are going to get Gina back and nail this bastard that I promise you, Patrick. We need to think and work out our strategy quickly."

Patrick nodded in agreement, then put his head down and ran his hands through his hair, like he was trying to massage this whole mess from his mind and body. His face had gone pink. He blew air from his mouth in an exasperated manner.

"I don't know how he will get Gina to Arthurs Seat unnoticed I mean it's a tourist spot near the capital. He must have some sort of plan, Patrick, something up his sleeve." Mike had ordered coffee from the police reception desk, the girl delivered a tray of coffee, milk and sugar, she also had the grace to not interrupt and leave the room promptly. Mike poured them both a strong coffee, they would need it.

"He must know that I am not going to offer him Tess? Even if I wasn't in the police I still couldn't do it." Patrick gulped down some coffee. The room was sickly warm, Patrick felt like the walls would crush him.

"Is that totally true Patrick? We have to start thinking along his lines, not our own. What is he expecting from us? Can we catch him out? Should we offer Tess? Or at least a double?" Mike only asked these questions as he and Patrick had been friends for years, otherwise Patrick would've punched him.

"I know Tess would do it. You have no idea how tormented she is from her own kidnap experience and from whatever the fuck happened even earlier to her. Yet she is brave. He would suspect a double. I am pretty certain he has watched Tess since the first time he fucking took her innocence in primary school. Fuck Mike, it makes me want to fucking puke. When we get him, he won't be making it to court. I have my very own court believe me." He swept hair from his forehead. Normally Patrick didn't fidget, he was robotic really, would've made a great poker player. This was all due to nerves and Mike new it too.

"Keep your cards close to your chest Patrick, very close, but I will always have your back." Mike smiled but it didn't reach his eyes.

They decided to send a team to survey Arthur's Seat, Tess would keep on working in the lab looking for evidence, safe with her boss David. They both decided that the Rookie would be in on their close-knit team, she had something about her. Patrick picked up his phone and summoned her.

The Rookie had never moved so fast in her life. She literally ran from the VCR room down towards the grander conference room. Officers parted ways as she ran through narrow corridors, she ignored her seniors warning her not to run. She paused at the door and knocked.

"Come in," Mike bellowed.

She entered and bowed her head in Patrick's direction.

"Sit down, sit down," Patrick said and gestured for her to do so. "Anything new?"

The Rookie bit her lip nervously, this was her big moment she couldn't fuck it up. She was just a council estate girl, now working on the biggest case in 2 countries.

"Tess's mum and dad are struggling to get a flight, covid and lack of staff," she said as she poured herself a coffee.

"Oh yes," said Mike, "it's always down to fucking politics. Pay airline staff the wages and they would have loads of staff."

The Rookie thought before opening her mouth, did she say what she had theorised or was she stupid?

"Sirs, I don't know what the plural is for two bosses, sorry." Now she felt stupid.

"That'll do fine, try not to fret with fucking inane practicalities," Patrick shrugged his shoulders his face like thunder, he nodded for her to carry on.

The Rookie twisted her hands nervously.

"Sirs, there's something in my memory, about politics, but I can't find what I'm looking for." She felt she was so sacked for naïve ineptitude.

"Politics?" asked Mike. "Go on."

The Rookie glanced at Patrick, daring not to hold his gaze too long.

"The guy we have footage on at the bookstore with Tess's book, he reminds me of a politician I've seen on TV. You see I watch Question Again with my dad, you know the show that debates politics? They have guest politicians and the guy looks familiar but I can't think who and the image isn't too clear."

Mike stifled a laugh. "What are you on about 20 and you watch politics?"

"Yes, yes sir. My dad is very political and we grew up on it, we watch it every Tuesday night if I'm not working."

Patrick rested his chin on his fist and looked at The Rookie with his piercing blue eyes.

"Ok, I need you to work all night, we need answers and leads. Can you bring in your dad? Show him the CCTV and see if he has any ideas? You are a fucking genius but have no confidence. You have spotted and noticed things where other time served officers haven't. I think you can help solve this and most importantly get my girl back to me."

Patrick took hold of her hands, circled them with his squeezed and nodded at her. She nodded back, stood up abruptly and went to work.

Skeletons Do Talk

Tess made a quick call to Jinty asking her to check on the flat, put the bins out and open her mail. She promised an increasingly alarmed Jinty that she would be fine and safe. They would catch up once she was home. She swiped off her phone, nodded to the police officer outside the lab who was staring at an image on what looked like a dating APP on his mobile. She entered the lab and could see David intently reading something on his laptop. He caught sight of Tess and stood up to greet her, which he did with the biggest of hugs. The starkness and clinical feeling of the lab made her feel safe; it's where she felt the most comfortable. She put on her lab coat and was grateful to see David had made up a big flask of tea and sandwiches for the nights work, he had also brought soup. He was a gem.

David pulled out the trolley containing the remains and used its breaking system to stabilise it in the centre of the room, there he lowered a huge lamp so they had better vision. They both pulled over moveable stools and positioned them to the correct height. David pulled his glasses from resting on his head to his eyes. They leaned forward without speaking and kept looking at the remains. Tess scraped her hair behind her ears. They had decided to excavate the skeleton in one piece, so had made cuts into the earth surrounding it and lifting it as one. She now lay on the trolley surrounded by decomposed earth.

At all times either Tess or David would take notes of exactly what they were doing and take photographs. It was difficult not to get drawn to the macabre sight of the foetal remains where the victim's womb had once been; life had surged through both the mother and child then just snuffed out. Tess wondered if the murderer new the victim was pregnant. Unless they had ambushed her it was unlikely an expectant mother wouldn't let on she was with child, almost like a bargaining tool, if so in this case the bargaining had failed. Tess shook her head to chase away these thoughts, they were just distracting her. They had removed earth from where the skull had been placed between the victim's legs, enabling them to lift the skull and place it on a separate examination table. With their brushes they dusted off dirt from the skull. They noticed an entry wound in the occiput. They exchanged glances, David then took more notes and while Tess photographed the wound. David wrote *Perimortem* in his notes.

David looked at Tess. Perimortem? It wasn't really a question as they both new what it was. Tess nodded. David added to his notes to make it clearer what they meant as police officers, lawyers and other non-scientist would also at some point be looking at their findings.

David had photographed each tooth and noted its identity before bagging them to be sent off for analysis. Data bases would be checked, dental records, anything that would lead to answers. From looking at the Pelvic bones they could see pock marks indicating a younger skeleton that established the victim to be about 20-35 years old. They narrowed down the age again by looking at the fusing of short bone caps and the end of the bone shafts called Epiphysis. They determined that the bones were still growing. They also noticed that the victim had breaks in both Tibias. She had obviously suffered trauma as a child as those breaks had healed themselves. Tess and David both sighed.

Tess twisted her mouth, "20 to 21 years old?"

David nodded and replied, "Also, it looks like she has given birth previously. Pretty young to have one child and another on the way."

Tess thought of Gina's mum. She cleared any thoughts of Gina, It would only distract from her job. David jotted down notes again and spoke so the laptops word dictate picked up what he was saying nothing apart from the injuries inflicted upon her suggested illness. Someone somewhere must be missing a child, niece, grandchild or sister. Come on he urged silently, give up your secrets. He brushed more earth from the left hand, the fist had been clenched, maybe from pain or maybe the victim had tried to hit her murderer. Something caught Dr Maclean's eye, it was an object in the fist that had caught the light. He drew down his powerful overhead light. Tess sensed the change in David, his energy shifted, she looked at him intensely.

The Politician

He didn't like performing tasks that he paid his staff to do, it was beneath him, demeaning. It should be the nannie's job. That awful inferior being had just sent him a text telling him to "stick his fucking job." This was quite inconvenient seeing as the school term was up. I mean he paid her well as a nanny, she only nannied full-time during the holidays as Mimmy was a full-time boarder. All the nanny had to do was make sure everything was supplied for Mimmy like clothing and ensure activities were booked and paid for, school fees, her horses were kept. Not any real nannying apart from the fucking holidays!

He grabbed his landline phone and dialled the number angrily. The house mistress answered immediately. He didn't do small talk and wasn't courteous.

"Mimmy's nanny has left I'm afraid so my chauffer will pick her up at 8AM prompt. Make sure she is ready as you know how I detest lateness."

With that he slammed down the phone. He really wished his brother would pay more attention to Mimmy, she was his daughter after all, it seemed that he was always clearing up his brother's messes.

The headmistress looked over at the sweet girl sat in the chair in her office, she swung her dangling legs, one with a cut to her knee which is why she was here. In fact she had fallen purposely so she could spend time with Dina the headmistress, for Dina was the light in Mimmy's miserable life. Mimmy's long blonde hair lay plaited over her shoulder, it was like spun gold. The child strode over to Dina and hugged her tightly.

"I don't want to spend the holidays with him. I want to stay with you, Dina."

A tear fell from Dina's eye, she wiped it away quickly.

"Child, believe me I am working on it. You might have to spend the first part of the holidays to appease him. Just annoy him and nosy into his business, he'll soon get bored of you I promise. Then we can head to the holiday cottage in Arran for a few weeks then down to mine in London. How would that be?"

Dina loved this child with love she had never known. She despised her brother, he was damn cruel, always had been. Mimmy was like her mother, Dina. Only Mimmy didn't know the connection yet. That would all be coming to an end soon though. Dina had to be strong, had to play this one out. Mimmy's life was at risk. How on earth she had suffered her brother's cruelty all those years she didn't know? Who could possibly stay with such a brother and keep their sanity? She had, had no choice but to leave Mimmy. Her brother was too powerful for Dina to fight on her own. She kissed Mimmy gently on her cheek "

"Soon, darling, soon we will all be together." Tears rolled down both their cheeks as they said a sad goodbye.

The Artist

As soon as he threw on any of his smoking jackets he felt powerful. Today he chose the dark red one which reeked of expensive clubs and art galleries. He glanced in the long antique mirror in his grand bedroom. He felt so very superior in every sense. Not good looking, but in a fashionable way he did possess that air of authority and breeding that you see in the upper classes of English nobility. He smirked at his reflection, opened the door and descended the sweeping staircase to the second floor. Here he entered the smoking room which he kept for just that. He sat in a dark green high backed Chesterfield chair. It sat on a handmade rug from the Middle East. It was somewhat frayed from age but this only added to its beauty and appeal. It's a shame you couldn't say the same about women he thought and stifled a laugh.

He pulled open the drawer of the walnut table that nestled against the chesterfield, took out a large immoderate cigar and lighter, lit the cigar and inhaled deeply. He stood and took a glass from his bar, poured a glass of a fine single malt whisky neat. He didn't understand how people could add coke or any other mixer? The same with a wine spritzer; it killed the taste which was most of the exciting part of alcohol. It must be a lower-class thing he chuckled.

He was getting a little bored with this game; it had lost its edge and excitement. He needed to rev it up and get back in control. He finished his cigar and whisky, savouring both. He left the smoking room and swept down to the first floor, he had the keys in his hand. There was a secret passage to that room. In fact during the *Rising of the North* in 1569 many priestly hiding holes were constructed in England, Wales and Ireland. The history of the Artist's castle wasn't so straightforward. His ancestors had lulled the priests into a false sense of security. Pretending to support the catholic Mary Queen of

Scots. They had lied and told the priests they would convert to Catholicism. An elaborate tunnel system was already in place so his ancestors could escape or hide. You had to really know the castle inside out to find this space. He felt along the wall and located the false partition. He pushed gently and a panel came loose. He made himself as small as he could to get through the hole, bearing in mind how small people had been during those times. Once through he descended down the first tunnel to his left, then the second one on his right, and finally the third one on his left. He had a large set of keys which he used to open the door. He entered and came to a corridor filled with different brightly coloured doors. These were deep underground now and the corridor resembled a dark rabbit warren. He took a large set of keys above the green door unlocked it and entered.

The room was so spiritual and grand; he loved the chandelier of bones and skulls. There were 20 priests' skeletons hanging from the chandelier. All had been lured here by his ancestors. The priests were promised safety, safe worship and a rite of passage. Instead what they encountered was hell on earth. They were bound, tortured, beaten and hung from the massive beams that held this warren together. They were shown no mercy.

The Artist picked up a long heavy Femur bone, it had been converted into an instrument of torture. Small pins had been embedded into one end a handle the other so you could grip while you assaulted your victim. It had been used as a torture implement on the priests, some would break betraying the whereabouts of other priests or convertors. Some would not and for that they would die a long lingering death. He loved the feel of it in his hands, the weight, the age and the work that had gone into crafting it. Gina blinked as the lights came on. She didn't have time to think as the object swung at her head.

The Father

Patrick was still in his meeting with Mike and the Rookie. They were exchanging ideas and theories, discussing the guy at the bookstore but nothing was going anywhere or leading to his daughter. The exchange between Tess and Gina would take place on Arthur's Seat, so the kidnapper had instructed. Patrick had serious doubts, how could anyone get to Arthur's Seat with his kidnapped daughter without raising suspicion? It didn't feel right, it was impossible. Add to that that the kidnapper would know they couldn't give up Tess. So what the fuck was this about? They had wasted hours thinking and debating. Then the lightbulb came on in Patricks head. His mobile rang disturbing his thought process, he answered abruptly.

"Yes, it's he."

His face fell. He picked up his coffee cup and smashed it against the wall.

Mike looked at the Rookie, she looked up to the ceiling as if in prayer. What the fuck was going on?

"He left my baby for dead, for fucking dead in a drugs den. She is barely alive my little girl, my little girl."

Mike looked at the Rookie and nodded for her to leave, she did so swiftly.

"Patrick, Patrick, you need to stay with me and strong ok. We need answers. First though let's go to Gina mate. Is she in Carlisle General?" Mike asked

"No she's in Glasgow General. She was found in Airdrie. I don't fucking understand how she ended up in Scotland." Patrick grabbed his coat and phone.

They ran through the long dreary corridors towards the exit and out to the waiting cars, as they passed the Rookie Mike nodded to her and said, "Carry on, girl." That was it but she knew what he meant.

Patrick and Mike jumped into the first police car with Patrick shouting "Go! Go! Go!" Not waiting for seatbelts to be clicked in or the usual formalities. Two other cars escorted them, blue lights flashing. The countryside flashed by at speed. It barely registered with Patrick.

A call came through on the Rookie's mobile, number unknown. She answered.

"Yes? Well I'm not sure really. Ok give me 10 minutes."

She picked up the car keys to her own car. She was technically just off-duty even though she would realistically give herself half an hour's time-out and then come back to the station. She questioned her actions but quickly dismissed them. She could justify her actions. She got in her car and drove to the rendezvous. As she pulled into the layby an image flashed in her brain. OMG! That's fucking it. I know who he is. Finally her brain had engaged and recognised where she had seen the kidnapper before. She picked up her phone and dialled Patrick. No answer. Damn! The car she had been waiting for pulled in front of hers. Fuck this would only take five minutes and she would call Patrick again as soon as this was over. She put her phone in her shoulder bag threw that over her arm, opened the car door and headed for the other car, a slight knot twisted in her stomach.

Patrick had, had no signal for a while. It was a bastard coming through the hills near the Lakes as the terrain was so high up. He had a missed call from the Rookie. He called back but no answer. He'd try again later, but now his mind lay elsewhere.

The Chauffeur

He pulled up outside the main office in the turning point of the school. The turning point was gravel where a large statue stood in the centre of the grounds. The statue was of a woman clutching a book. It was the school's founder Michaela Higgins. He beeped his horn impatiently.

Dina escorted Mimmy out of the door, she stopped and hugged her tightly again, and gain they both wept. He beeped the horn again and glared at Dina. She scowled at him. Mimmy opened the back door and Dina fastened her safely in. Dina then wrapped on the driver's window. He looked up pressed the widow down slowly. Dina spat in his face. Mimmy couldn't stifle her laugh.

"I'm fucking warning you, I don't want to hear or see you these holidays alright, quit fucking laughing."

God he hated females, all ages, all colours. All of them. He had no problem serving his master, he idolised him and would do anything he asked. Like getting rid of the cop's girl today. Left her in some rotten drugs den to be raped. His master had purposely left her barely alive, it was no accident or stupidity on his part, it merely excited him. If his master had wanted the girl dead, she would be dead by now. He was disappointed as he would've loved killing the copper's daughter, taken great delight and time in his executing work. He stuck his foot hard on the accelerator so the little girls head jerked back, one day he would like to snap it like a twig, horrible little twat.

Skeletons Do Talk

Tess continued to observe David and his intense concentration. He had the smallest pair of tweezers she had ever seen. He entered the curled up skeleton fist and pinched something between them. He gently pulled it out from the grasp of death

"Oh," is all Tess could muster

David laid it out on the table. It was delicate but obviously a bracelet. For a while he dare not touch it, he was scared to do so, as if it would disintegrate before they had time to study it. Tess pulled on her glasses and angled the lamp nearer the jewellery. She wrote down the item in the itinerary: Example number 1.

She moved it with her own tweezers, laying it out, she could see it was expensive. It was more solid bracelet rather than one with a chain. It had lots of diamonds embedded but she was not a jewellery expert, in fact she barely wore any. On the front was an engraved bar. Tess glanced up at David. The engraving consisted of a female skeleton draping over the bones of a swan! Tess let out a gasp, for more reasons than one.

"It's a Cartier, Tess. I mean how much would something like this cost?" he asked and looked at Tess for guidance. All he had ever bought was high street jewellery for his boyfriend, neither bothered about materialistic items.

She raised her eyebrows in mock sarcasm. Like she would fucking know. David laughed. They would make the best team ever he thought. Tess's face turned serious, she got her brush and brushed away soil that obstructed the front of the bracelet. It was hard to make out the engraving but when she did she stepped back and gasped. The world closed in on her, the rabbit hole tried to suck her in. Tess gripped the side of her chair; she took deep breaths, slowly inhaling as she put her head between her knees. David had his hand on her back rubbing gently.

"Slowly, Tess, slowly," he said as he wiped sweaty hair from her brow.

Tess began to regain her composure, she was learning to control her panic attacks, often she teetered on the edge of the rabbit hole but she knew now if she fell in she was in trouble, but if she tried to control the situation she had a little control over her life.

She sat up tentatively, carefully as David had retrieved fresh water from the changing area and handed it to her. Tess gulped eagerly. She was so dry. She raised a hand letting David know that she had it under control.

"Sorry David, thank you. Do you have a cigarette?"

He frowned at her while trying to smile at the same time. He went back into the changing area and pulled a cigarette from his backpack then hurried back to Tess.

"Two minutes," she said as she dashed out of the lab into the changing area and out the door.

The Rookie And The Cop

Before she got out of her car she'd tried to text Patrick about what she had remembered. The text failed to send, weak signal. She decided she would call 999 as it was imperative she got hold of Patrick or someone else at least. Fuck! Fuck! Fuck! Her phone ran out of charge. Too late now. She opened the door and got into the passenger seat.

"Where's your car? And don't be long."

She looked sideways at him not really wanting to be here or in the same breathing space. She heard the crack of the Taser. She didn't even have time to register her shock.

The Cop sat there for a few minutes contemplating what he had just done. Drool escaped the side of the rookie's mouth where she was leaning sideways against the passenger door. She was totally incapacitated. How he'd love to fuck her right now but that was out of the question, all that DNA shit. Instead, he opened her shirt with his gloved hand, into her bra and squeezed her breast hard. He would wait until he got home and have sex with his girlfriend while thinking about the Rookie, cocky little bitch. She had ruined his career, nearly his relationship. He had lied to his girlfriend as to why he was suspended but rumour got out like it always did in that shitty little town. Mind you, his girlfriend was shit scared of him anyhow so he supposed no real threat of her leaving him. She was timid and mousy, it was like fucking a doormat. God, now he was getting hard just thinking about fucking the Rookie. He would just have to make sure there was no DNA left, at all.

He pulled out the rookies bobble that held her hair in that boring cop neat bun. It cascaded over her shoulders like a dark waterfall,

all wavy and shiny. Fucking hell she was hot, even hotter when she couldn't speak. She had started to become aware a little. He raised his hand and slapped her face with the back of his hand, he chuckled, the power felt immense. He licked her face from jaw to temple, then grabbed her head to face him and stuck his tongue in her mouth. He dropped one hand into his own trousers and started to fondle himself.

The Rookie played dead, or rather immobile. She had started to gain consciousness when he slapped her. Confused she closed her eyes while trying to figure out what was going on. She would bide her time and wait until he was at his weakest. Suddenly he let her go jumped out of the car and opened her passenger door. She was going to make a move when the Taser hit her again, her head involuntarily jerking while her body reacted to the shock.

The Cop dragged her down a nearby embankment and propped her up against a tree. He paced through the undergrowth, thick from the summer's heat, he needed time to think. If the fucking bitch hadn't started this and that bastard Patrick hadn't suspended him then she wouldn't be in this situation, none of this was his fault. He had to kill her he knew that. He wasn't struggling with any of this, far from it. An owl flew overheard and made him jump, he shuddered, he hated birds, bats anything that could fly. Oh fuck, her phone, he would have to get it and dump it elsewhere to throw his colleagues off track, they would be looking for her at some point.

He strode over to where he had left her, he would get the phone then rape her, bury her whatever, they might even think it's something to do with the case. He leant over her and felt her pockets found her phone and pulled it out of her trouser pocket, lingering a little too much. He felt her breath on his face, then felt something jagged hit the side of his skull. Upon impact he dropped her phone put his hand to his head and felt blood. He regained his composure just enough to see the Rookie crawling away, crawling as fast as she could for her life. He went for his Taser, where the fuck was it? He must've dropped it. He threw himself forward and landed near her feet, grasping and grabbing at her frantically. She kicked out, hitting him in the shoulder but not enough to curb him. He grabbed again this time he got her boot, he held on tightly as she kicked out again and again, then she shook her foot out of the boot and scrambled frantically to her knees.

It was dark but not pitch black, a little moonlight shone down, she was not sure if that was a hindrance or a help. She had lost a boot in the struggle and her foot painfully snagged on brambles. She tried not to cry out, she had to remain as calm as she possibly could. He had taken her phone, not that it was any use anyway without any fucking charge. She half ran half fell down a steep gorge, trees stopping her from falling all the way down. Although her body hi some them causing jolts of temporary pain, adrenalin was kicking in.

She thought she heard something behind her and panicked. She got down on her side and rolled the rest of the way. He thought he heard her. He had a flashlight, though he struggled to get it on, he put out his palm and hit it with the flashlight, something reconnected and the light flickered on. Result, he had better sight now. He came upon a steep gorge, for a second he didn't think she would have the stamina to take this route, the terrain was steep, the ground uneven and covered in thick under-bush. Trees and stumps littered their way down the gorge making it even more perilous. His light caught sight of a figure, it was her. She had rested near a tree and looked to be out of breath or getting her bearings. She dropped to the ground quickly then he lost sight of her. It didn't really matter; she had one boot on and was slow from the Taser, a river stood in her way at the bottom of the gorge. There was nowhere for her to go. He had hiked up here in years gone by, to the left of the river the land rose steeply, it was a place where rock climbers liked to practice, so dead end for her. He laughed at that, literally a dead end. If she went right the path would lead her miles away from the road, if she deviated from it she would have to tackle more dense forest and growth. Eventually she would hit open moorland but that would take her hours.

"Rookie, come on let's talk," he barely raised his voice as he knew she would hear him. The silence in this gorge was deafening. He carried on forward his head throbbing instead of his manhood.

She was on the bank of the river, it was pretty fast flowing from the heavy rain that morning. She stopped long enough to think. Slowly she climbed down the steeper part of the bank, grabbing hold of roots from some old tree system she lowered herself in the water. Although the summer had been hot so far, it was night time and the water felt freezing, she let her body adjust then half swam while pulling herself along with various root systems always making contact with the embankment. She saw the flashlight above her took a deep breath and ducked under the dark water, all the time travelling towards the steep rock face.

Queens Hospital, Glasgow

As soon as the car pulled up Patrick raced to reception bursting through its doors that shook in aftershock. The receptionist looked up quickly though not in alarm like she was used to it. Momentarily the harsh fake light of the hospital made Patrick blink, the stark whiteness of everything, the walls, ceiling and desk didn't help matters.

"My daughter Gina. Gina," . . . he expelled air from his lungs while blinking away tears.

The receptionist leaned over and put her hand on Patrick's arm in a comforting gesture. Lesley, read the receptionist's name tag. Lesley typed something into her computer just for clarification really. She already knew that the girl had come in in a pretty bad state that she was in intensive care.

"Intensive care, level 3, ward 6. Take the next right then lift 1'," she said as she paged the Doctor as she instructed Patrick.

Patrick ran to towards the lift, smacking his hand against the button willing the lift to hurry up. He didn't wait for people to alight instead he barged through them and started pressing for level 3. A man was about to confront Patrick but having seen the look on his face decided against it. The lift seemed to take ages to get to its destination, he wondered if death row felt like this when the prisoners walked their last walk. He felt sick with trepidation and sweating so much perspiration ran down the side of his face.
A doctor was waiting and extended out his hand, Patrick took his quickly, eager to get the formalities done with.

"Where is she? I need to see her," he almost whispered.

The doctor nodded kindly, "First, let's just take the family room and I will tell you what's going on."

He led Patrick to a small side room. The room was stark, but how could it not be when people were this close to death? Two chairs and a sofa were arranged round a coffee table, the suite were a dull grey. Tea and coffee making facilities plus a water dispenser sat on a work surface at the back of the room. A few magazines lay on the coffee table, like people would give a fuck what was in fashion or which celebrity was fucking which in a situation like this. Life goes on. The doctor gestured towards the refreshments, but Patrick shook his head.

"Ok, so your daughter Gina," he glanced at his notes. "She took some blunt force trauma to the top of her head, although this looks worse than it is, so don't panic when you first see her. The worst thing was actually the cocktail of drugs, I mean we have concluded she is not nor has ever been a user?" He glanced at Patrick for confirmation.

Patrick sucked in air and shook his head angrily.

"Thought so, we had little information when she came in. She came in as a potential overdose not as a kidnap victim. It soon became apparent even before clarification from the police that she wasn't a user."

He checked to see if Patrick was following before continuing. "The concoction she was given was harmful, but it was like someone knew what they were doing. She was given heroin, cocaine, tramadol and alcohol. She has pneumonia and is very dehydrated. She was lucky the drug's den was raided otherwise she might not have made it. We are seeing signs of her coming round and her vitals are much better. I will take you to see her," the doctor concluded and stood up. Patrick followed him down the long narrow corridor, the lights as harsh as they were in the reception hurting his eyes, the bleeps from machines sounding as they kept patients alive, that sound would never leave Patrick's ears. They rounded a corner into the intensive care unit. When Patrick caught a glimpse of Gina he was as close as he had ever been to collapsing.

Skeletons Do Talk

Still a little high from the nicotine fix, Tess looked at the engraving and then at David, back to the engraving and back to David again. David rubbed his forehead and looked back at Tess. They had brushed away more dirt and grime to reveal the full engraving.

D, I offer you, in flesh and blood my one true love

"Who is D?" David asked.

Tess leant over the bracelet and studied the engraving.

"I was never sure David, but that bracelet was made for me, and I wore it. Fancy a smoke?' David winked and off they went.

David lit up first then offered Tess a light, she lit up and inhaled deeply.

"I lied," she said, that's all she said she didn't elaborate.

"About what, Tess?" David asked between coughing and smoking. She let his coughing fit pass before she explained. The moon was out partially, she thought about who it might be shining on now, what they might be doing?

"The day I was kidnapped my mum and dad had gone out, a delivery man knocked, I Said he just asked if mum and dad were in as he had a package and when I said they weren't in the man said he couldn't leave the package and left." She glanced sideways at David.

"Go on," he said.

She took a long deep drag. She would regret smoking in the morning especially if she went for a run.

"The man gave me a package and told me to open it when he had left. Of course he asked if mum and dad were home. He said if I wanted to meet D then I should take a walk later, up to the fields where the houses gave way to the countryside. I fancied a boy at school called Dylan. He had left little notes and posted them through my locker. He fancied me too. He would sign off D, most likely to save embarrassment should I tell my friends, he could remain anonymous. Anyhow I thought it was him." She gave a nervous laugh

"God teenagers, even though I had been kidnapped and God knows what I was still too embarrassed to mention this in case it got back to Dylan. The bracelet was in the package, I kind of knew in my heart that Dylan who was just a schoolboy couldn't afford anything as fancy as that, but I ignored my gut feeling. I took the dog for a walk that night and wore my bracelet with pride, I'm not sure at which point during the kidnap it came off and I never mentioned it until now." She stubbed her cig out against the wall.

"Where's Dylan now?" asked David.

She shrugged.

"Why? The last I heard he was still in Leeds. He married a girl from school and they have two kids." She started walking back towards the lab.

"I think we should track him down and give him a call, just to rule him out." He looked at his watch and pulled a funny face, it was past 1AM. They stayed in the changing rooms while looking for

Dylan on Facebook, they found him and his mobile was public. They used David's mobile to call and put it on speaker. On the third ring a very groggy not so happy voice answered.

"Hello, this better be good."

David introduced them both and explained.

"Fucking hell, Tess. Tess O'Brien?"

They heard someone else in the background and Dylan reassuring her.

"Sorry, it's late and my wife was curious. Well, I certainly didn't buy the bracelet. Sorry to say Tess. Yes I left the notes but only as some bloke collared me near school, said he was your cousin and asked me to leave them. I mean fucking hell, Tess you were hot man, but what, two school years below me? No way would I've dared ask you out, but the bloke paid me to do it. Ouch!" Again they heard a woman in the background this time she sounded angry.

"Fuck you Dylan, Tess fucking O'Brien was a fucking geek, I'll sleep with the kids tonight." Followed by more muffled arguing.

"Ok, thanks for that, Dylan. Really. The police might want a statement at some point. In fact call them now and give a description if you can." Tess hung up.

"I can't believe I ever fancied him," she said as she stuck her fingers down her throat.

"Tess, I used to fancy Philip Schofield. I totally understand."

They had a good laugh before changing back into their PPE. David entered the lab while Tess hung back to call Patrick. She spoke briefly to get an update on Gina, poor girl, Jesus. She popped her phone back into her bag in her locker then walked towards the lab, she had Déjà vu, something to do with Dylan. She couldn't quite put her finger on it but she didn't think he had told her the whole truth.

The Rookie

John tried calling his daughter's mobile. No answer. He imagined she would be working over, especially with Gina's kidnapping, although she usually answered. He called the station just to be sure. Connie was on front desk tonight, she answered the phone with her usual dour manner.

"Hi, it's John, Kristen's dad. Can I just speak to her if she is available, please?' Connie rolled her eyes, she had better things to do than chase round after the Rookie, she called different departments, mmm, and she wasn't in the station. Connie checked the carpark cameras, she couldn't see the Rookie's car either.

"Hey John, She's not here nor is her car. Could've sworn she was supposed to be back, I'll call the other lass who was on desk duty and see if she said anything to her. I'll put you on hold one sec." She didn't wait for him to answer she pressed 9 for an outside line and spoke to her colleague.

"Hey John thanks for waiting, well this is a little odd, she said she had to go off for a quick meeting at the end of her shift, but she was coming back to work on the case, her car isn't in the carpark so she must've taken it but its quarter past 1 and she should've been back about 11.30. She didn't have a date, did she?"

They were all the same these youngsters, not exclusive they called it, in her day it was slutty.

John started to get worried, this wasn't like her at all.

"Ok Connie and no she didn't have a date. The job comes first especially with all that's happening I'm calling Patrick." He hung up abruptly.

Matteus And Elouise

Music blared from the car speakers, cool dance but Elouise couldn't remember who it was. Mat was driving fast, Matteus was his real name, he was Latvian and worked on the fishing boats, much cooler and fitter than boys her own age. They had been to a party and were off their heads on E. Matt was weaving fast along the winding country lanes. They would find a place to park and make out. Elouise pulled down the interior mirror and clicked on a light, she ruffled her stunning blond hair and pouted her naturally full lips admiring her reflection. She didn't know who was more beautiful, her or Matt. She applied lip gloss looked over at Matt and smiled seductively. Matt winked. They normally pulled into a lay buy up at the top of Devil's gorge. Matt was about to pull in but two cars were already parked; one cars passenger door was wide open. Matteus pulled in behind the dark blue Vauxhall.

"Matt, fucking drive somewhere else," Elouise pleaded.

"Shhh," he chastised, which infuriated her. She hit his thigh.

"Oi, Elouise, it's weird. I just want to make sure no one is injured."

"And I just want to make out!" She was furious and tossed her blond hair over her shoulder and pouted her best pout. "If someone's hurt what then? We are off our fucking skulls on E."

He ignored her put on the brake and got out of the car.

"Get the torch, it's on your side," he motioned to the dashboard.
Elouise found It, as she went to hand it to Matt she licked it suggestively. He shook his head and laughed; she really was something else, a firecracker they might call her in English.

The moon although not full was shining down brightly, it eerily lit up the forest, trees looked they might start to come alive, or was that the E working its magic? Matt walked towards the blue car with the open passenger door and shone his torch back and forth, back and forth, looking for who the fuck knew? He strode to the next car; a little black mini, it was unlocked. He shone his torch inside the car, keys in the ignition. This was getting stranger; he looked about in the car for anything. The car was spotless. In the glove compartment was a bag of unopened sweets, sour dinosaurs. He rummaged about a bit more, logbook but nothing else. He pulled down the mirror above the driver's seat, oh a wallet of some sort. He put on the car's interior light to get a better look, startled he dropped the wallet, picked it up again looked again. He was worried now. He put the Id in his pocket and shut the car door very quietly. He stopped again at the blue Vauxhall. Something caught his eye just under the car. He stooped down picked it up then stood up again wiping dirt from his trousers with his free hand. He shone the torch over the object, curiosity took the better of him and he squeezed the button on whatever he was holding, it zapped loudly. He jumped and nearly dropped it. He looked around him at this pretty desolate place and fear crept up his neck and prickled his skin, like the devil was caressing him. He ran to his car closed the doors and locked them. He turned to Elouise.

"Fucking hell babe, something's really bad. Call the police."

"What? No! No! We've taken fucking drugs, babe."

At that he showed her the police ID and the Taser gun. Her eyes went wide, her skin turned ghostly white. She dialled 999 and told him to drive.

"Drive, get the fuck out of here," she screamed.

The Rookie

The Rookie heard him searching for her, so she bobbed down into the water but stayed still. When she no longer heard him, she pressed on towards the rocks. She was freezing but the adrenaline rushed through her veins willing her on. It was hard work as she was going against the current, debris kept catching her, threatening to take her under to the depths of death. She held on tightly to roots on the verge, resting for a moment when she came to a tree, she clung on praying.

The Cop was now at the river bank, he looked right and left listening all the time and shining his torch. The Rookie was a tough lass, and intelligent so she would probably try being one step ahead of him. 50/50 left or right. He tried to think like her, what would she do? She would go left as she would think he would think she would take the right. Although what she would do when she got to the waterfall and rock face he didn't know. Maybe he could catch her and drown her? No one knew they had met. He rushed on now, through tough brush and undergrowth, finally he got to a point where the undergrowth relented, he breathed a little bit, he heard something in the water, could be an otter maybe? Then he heard her, he heard her cough, he shone his torch into the river, as the light hit, something submerged itself. He picked up some rocks and threw them at the invisible target, her head and shoulders came out of the water, and she let out a screech like a wounded animal.

"Must be cold in there honey. I'm here all night so maybe give it up and get out now?" He threw another rock; he heard the sick thud as it connected with flesh.

She stopped stunned, she could feel the blood running down her face, she took deep breaths to compose herself. If she stayed on this side she would die, either by stoning or freezing. She was a strong swimmer but the river was wide and fast.

"I'm not your fucking honey," she yelled, with that with all the force she could muster she propelled herself forward and across the raging river

Tess 2006

Tess, Laura and Fizzy were getting ready for the youth club, excitement filled Tess's bedroom as Nelly Furtado blasted out of Tess's music station singing about being promiscuous. The girls giggled as Fizzy, nicknamed because she was constantly bubbly and fizzing about, picked up the end of a skipping rope and mimed to the song while gyrating her hips. The door flew open and Tess's mum stood there.

"Girls, I'm not sure this song is appropriate, hurry up."

She smiled as she chastised them. The girls followed as did a plume of too strong perfume. Tess was the last out, ever the conscientious girl she turned out the lights and flipped the music off. As she closed her door a poster flew off on to the bedroom floor, not the poster you might imagine in a teenagers room, this was a map of known archaeological sites in Yorkshire.

Tess's parents would take them to the youth club, it was their turn at having all the girls over. Each set of parents took it in turn every Friday night. As the girls were going to the youth club, all the parents were meeting for a meal and wine, well not Tess's mum Carol, she wouldn't be drinking as she was designated driver this weekend.

When Carol pulled up outside the youth club the girls almost fell out of the car in a pile they were so eager to get in or too embarrassed to be seen with parents?

"Hey girls, 10 o'clock no later ok?" Jason, Tess's dad shouted after them. He shouldn't have bothered, they either didn't hear or didn't listen, and they hurtled towards the club like a racehorse over the winning line. Jason and Carol laughed as they drove off, they adored these girls.

The girls waited until Tess's parents were out of sight then hitched up their skirts a few notches, sorted out each other's hair then entered the youth club. First they played pool, then bought chips and coke and devoured those in minutes. Oh, more Nelly Furtado, the girls ran to the dance floor as *Maneater* blasted out of the speakers. The girls danced awkwardly and a little self-consciously, not yet teenagers, not really children. They were only 12 but already Tess was blooming, the others not far behind, they sang loudly to *Maneater* and knew all the words but failed to realise what the song was really about; still innocent.

Tess tossed back her long blond hair, as she did she caught glimpse of much older boys. They were stood near the girls toilets trying to look as cool as possible which they managed in their baggy jeans, expensive trainers and attitude. One resembled Eminem, he had the same swagger and cockiness. He caught sight of Tess and stared at her while chewing gum. It was a different stare than just a stare, she felt embarrassed, her cheeks burning as she turned away she thought he had winked at her. She re-joined her friends singing to *Maneater*, in seconds it seemed Fizzy had gained lots of confidence and now jumped about while miming. Tess glanced over at the older boys again trying not to be too obvious. She was pretty sure they were drinking alcohol. A tall boy with a prominent Adam's apple and spotty complexion was topping up their cokes with something out of his pocket. An older girl strode over to the group of boys, she had on white hot pants, trainers and a t-shirt, she was extremely pretty. She approached 'Eminem' and went in to kiss him but he pushed her away. She shouted something at him that Tess couldn't hear but you didn't have to be a lip reader to have a vague idea of what she said.

"I'm just going to the loo," she shouted to her friends, who didn't take a blind bit of notice. She patted the back of her kilt like skirt to make sure it wasn't too short, or too long. As she sauntered in the direction of the loos she realised 'Eminem' was no longer with the group. As she went to enter the toilets, the taller boy with the Adam's apple part blocked her entrance.

"Excuse me please," she had mustered all her strength to utter those words. *Bad Day* came on and blared from the nearby speakers. The boy glowered down at her, she thought he maybe about 6ft. 2 in, as his face got closer to hers she started to sweat, he smelled of booze.

"Fucking jail bait," he spat out. "You think Dylan fancies you? You?" he reiterated. "Fucking idiot," he said as he moved out of her way.

"Thank you," she replied without looking up.

She took the first grey dingy toilet cubicle and locked herself in. She had to grow a backbone, things would get much worse the older she got, the older kids could be really nasty. She did a pee quickly, relieved she hadn't got her period. Maybe it was because she'd just started there was no regular pattern, but she found if she got worried or stressed sometimes it would bring one on. It was cold in here even though the summer was a scorcher, it could be the cold tiles or lack of light as the toilets had no windows, she shivered and heard footsteps as she flushed the loo. She had a big smile on her face as she exited the toilet ready to swap pleasantries or lipstick with the girls who had come in. She made her way to the cracked wash basin then stood dead in her tracks, "What are you doing in here?" Panic began to coarse through her veins

Skeletons In My Closet

For the last 6 hours Patrick and Mike had been at Gina's bedside. Remarkably in that time she had made great progress. Patrick had just got off the phone, Tess had called worried about both him and Gina. He had brought her up to date and asked her to get regression therapy as soon as she could. He was still a little annoyed at her, actually really pissed at her. She had wasted valuable time and he didn't know if she simply didn't remember or didn't want to? There was a big difference.

"Patrick," Mike put his hand on Patrick's arm and nodded towards Gina.

"Dad," Patrick rushed towards his daughter, knelt down and kissed her cheek. Mike passed a baby like cup with a straw filled with water. Gina sipped slowly and grimaced as she did. She looked at her dad then Mike, the two most important people in her life, especially since her gran had died. A large vase of baby's breath stood on the cabinet, Gina's favourite.

"Do I look like shit?" she asked them both, Gina would always be the same.

"No," they both chorused in unison not daring to tell her the truth. Her head had been shaved where she had been hit, so the surgeons could access the damage. Fucking hell the shit would hit the fan when she saw that.

Mike stepped forward and carefully gave her a hug.

"Ginie, as soon as you feel up to it, we need as much information as you can remember."

He could barely stand seeing her like this; he still called her Ginie as that's what she would call herself as a toddler when she couldn't pronounce her own name.

"Do you think I could speak to the Rookie cop? It might be easier," she asked, looking at them both she showed vulnerability.

"If that's what you want," Patrick said worriedly. He wondered why she had requested the female cop. If that fucker had touched her in any way . . . He gripped the under the bed so Gina couldn't see his knuckles turn white. Mike had read his mind and placed his hand on Patricks shoulder, both in a reassuring gesture and a 'hold your horses mate.

"I'll grab a couple of coffees and call the rookie," Mike said "Although she was supposed to be keeping us in the loop and updated? I wonder if she didn't want to disturb us, she's a nice kid."

Mike had only met her a few times but he was impressed with the Rookie, she was so young but very dedicated.

"Yes she is, call her, Mike and get her to drive up here pronto, I'll take a strong coffee please mate."

Patrick couldn't shake a bad feeling, as if someone just walked over his grave. As Mike left the room Patrick's mobile sounded, "One sec Gina," he said as he went into the corridor. A nurse walked past mouthing at him for having his phone on at all, she also made a cut throat gesture. He just glared at her. He answered his phone, finally.

"Hey, it's Patrick." His face broke out first in confusion, then in anger as he listened to John.

"John, she's what? Missing? My colleague was just about to call her."

Fucking hell could anything else go wrong? Another call was coming through.

"Leave it with me and my team, John,. She won't be far and we'll find her, ok?' He swiped that call off and answered the other incoming call. It was the station.

"Boss, oh boss, it's Connie from the station.

"Where the fuck is the Rookie? I've just had her dad on the phone," Patrick was shouting, though Connie knew him well enough to know it wasn't personal.

"Boss, we've just had a call come in from a terrified young couple. They found the Rookie's ID, a Taser on the ground, the Rookie's car, which was unlocked, and an unidentified car. Both abandoned." He could hear her suck in air, like it would somehow help.

"Fucking hell Con, what's going on? Gina is awake and wants to talk but not to me or Mike. She wants the Rookie. I can't tell her the Rookie is missing it'll be too much for her."

He had never felt at a loss in his job like he did now. It felt like the walls were closing in on him.

"Boss, my shift has finished but I'll drive up and talk to Gina, she'll talk with me. If you can Boss, we need you and Mike down here ok? I'll grab my coat and I'm on my way." With that Connie handed over her shift, grabbed her coat and drove breaking every speed limit in the two countries.

As Patrick headed back to speak with Gina, Mike flew round the corner, dripping two coffees as he went.

"You heard?" Mike asked Patrick, although he knew by his face he had.

The Hunted

She swam with all her might all her strength all her being, debris kept snagging her legs like tendrils from an octopus were trying to drag her under. The water was fast and ferocious so she could barely hear anything but the whooshes and burbles, really she should be on her back doing backstroke to retain any body heat, but she didn't have the time for the slower stroke, she needed the power of front crawl. That meant most of her body was submerged even partially, which led to a drop in body temperature. Out here in the open countryside as soon as the sun went down the temperature dropped rapidly, it was unforgiving. She pushed on against the current, which was taking its toll, she felt her stomach rumble, she hadn't eaten and the calories she had burned must've been huge. She would kill for a fish and chips with scraps on, slightly greasy with tonnes of salt and vinegar. That was her aim, she would aim to have a fish and chip supper tomorrow night with her Da, her beautiful Irish Da. Just thinking about him made her push on even faster, like she had a second wind, she thought about her mum, standing at the side of the pool cheering her on, then later worriedly watching her daughter sea swimming. Her lovely, sweet mum dead, a drunk driver slamming into her body killing her instantly. She heard her mum louder now, like she was really with her, "Come on baby girl," and then, "fucking swim, swim as fast as you can baby girl, he's going to kill you." She took a breath, put her face in the water and drove on and on, diagonal and upwards, the wounds from the rocks he threw were like painful crosses she had to bare and drag with her.

The Cop watched her. She had taken a few hits with the rocks which had slowed her considerably. He swung the flashlight just to double check there were no stray campers or tourists. The woodland was dark and menacing, gnarled and twisted trunks and branches looked like they would come alive and engulf your soul. He stripped to his boxers. He would leave his clothes and trainers hidden in the undergrowth, once he had got rid of her he would come back and get dressed. He wouldn't take the car it wasn't registered to him anyway, but precaution was the best policy. He would then hike home, just an innocent hiker nothing more. He glanced down at his perfect body, any woman would be privileged to see it or touch it, yet that bitch had got him suspended. He acclimatised to the cold water, getting in waist deep, before plunging into the darkness, his strong arms propelling him faster than hers.

He didn't hear the car in the distance pull up, or the girl screaming. She made it to the pool, the Fairy Pools of Devil's Mouth locals called it. In summer the pools were so pretty with the waterfall cascading down, everything surrounding them were so green. The moss, the trees and the lichen letting you know you breathed in purity. The rock face though, well that was something else. The bottom jutted out like a jagged chin, the rest appeared face shaped, the Devil's Mouth got its name from the rock formation and the danger, countless people had lost their lives either falling after free climbing or diving into the pools below on to rocks that you that couldn't be seen from the top.

She hoped she wouldn't become a statistic. She almost fell on to the bottom of the rock face she was so exhausted. She took a moment to compose herself and then viewed the vertical nightmare she would have to navigate. She had rid herself of her remaining boot when entering the river and was now barefoot. The jagged rock surface would tear her feet to ribbons, she unhooked her padded bra, she pulled out the cushions that gave her the uplift effect she desired to be a double EE so there was a lot of padding material. She always carried hair bobbles on her wrist as she wasn't allowed to wear her hair down at work just in case they snapped she had a bracelet of them. She attached each bra pad to the soles of her feet using the bobbles to secure them. That would give her feet a little protection. She could hear the waterfall cascading down and speckles of water hit her face and body, she heard something behind her; HIM, he was catching up. Her heart hammered in her chest and she tried to ignore the palpitations, she blew and blew out of her mouth to stave crying. Then she launched herself up the Devil's jawline, carefully picking the right spots to place her feet and grasp the next ledge. She glanced back to see him enter the Fairy Pools, like the Devil himself he laughed and mocked her. He stood in the Fairy Pool watching her climb for her life. He would go after her but first he would have some more fun.

"Hey honey, I was really good at the fairground games when I was younger."

He picked up a rock, its edges spiked out angrily.

"You know Can Alley, target shot, used to impress the girls, yes so much that I got laid all the time."

He juggled the rock from one hand to the other, the weight of it made him feel powerful.

"Not you though hey? Bolted at the fucking knees, I've had girls like you, forced 'em. They all screamed the same WHA WHA WHA, but they enjoyed it, They enjoy it even more now I have the uniform. Just come down and we can come to some sort of arrangement if you know what I mean."

Nothing, she didn't utter a fucking word, little bitch.

She hugged the rock face as he shouted up to her. Crazy bastard. She took a deep breath as he called her a bitch and she searched for her next footing, she found a nook enough to fit her left foot into, with her right she felt for another nook or pocket anything to get her foothold. Yes she found another one, the bra padding saving her from the rawness of the rock's edges. She took another deep breath, kept her body hugging close to the rocks, she pushed up with her feet, her hands searching for cracks in the rock like lizards trying to escape the heat in some hot foreign country. Her right hand found a crevice, she counted to three and then her left hand felt for another. Fuck, Oh my fucking God! something hit her left hand, excruciating pain shot through the small bones in her hand and shock waves went to her fingers, she loosened her grip from the crevice just as her left hand found a shelf to hang on to. Her right hand fell away wafting in the cool night's breeze. The motion nearly made her lose any grip she had on the devils mouth. She blinked back tears her hand felt like it was broken. She tried to ignore the pain and compose herself. She felt again with the only hand she could, the shelf was much deeper than she had thought, maybe a platform, she was trying to remember the rock formation from her summer picnics here.

She felt a little relief, that's it, there were 2 platforms that looked like eyes, big enough for a person her size to get into or rest on. With every ounce of courage and strength she could muster she heaved herself up, using her bad hand too which nearly made her sick with pain. She got on her tiptoes which made her feel taller. Finally she could put both elbows on the platform as leverage. She heaved herself up, her lower body feeling like a concrete weight trying to anchor her to her death. She breathed out as she pushed herself straight into the eye of the Devil. She rested then started to think about the rest of her climb, the Devil had a prominent brow that jutted out pretty far. She wasn't sure how on earth she could gage it especially with her broken hand. She thought back to earlier on this summer, climbing and Gyhll Scrambling with her friend. They had done this climb freestyle many times, during daylight; in fact they had sat at the top of the Devil many times. Her friend Ellidah lived just over the Scottish border in tiny village. They could almost see her village on a clear day. She wondered what Ellidah was doing now, if she would ever see her again? That made her sad. She had a massive crush on her. She snapped out of her thoughts when she heard him scaling the rock face.

She spoke to herself telling herself to be calm, breath, just like she told people when she attended road traffic accidents or domestic abuse incidents, easier said than done, she had to think quickly.

Skeletons In My Closet

Connie arrived at Glasgow Queens Hospital about an hour and a half after she had got off the phone with Patrick. She had stopped at the garage to refuel picking up various beauty items for Gina, oh she knew Gina too well and she would be worrying about her hair and skin more than anything. She grabbed two teas on her way past the hospital canteen then headed towards Gina's ward.

Gina had been moved from ICU to a side ward where she was the only bed in the room thank God. A police officer sat on a chair by the entrance of her room, cutting a very sombre figure. She retrieved her ID and showed it to him before he had time to request it. He just nodded and smiled a small smile.

Gina had been sleeping but woke upon hearing someone enter her room, on seeing Connie she started to weep. Connie held out her ample arms and body and gave Gina the big hugs Gina had grown accustomed to from her for since she was a child. Gina's nanna and Connie were Gina's maternal figures, damn good strong ones. Gina smelled Connie's familiar cheap coconut hair conditioner and even cheaper bargain basin perfume, along with cigarette smoke, she breathed in that smell never wanting to forget it. She held Connie tightly, Connie reciprocated.

"Ok, enough snot madam," said Connie wiping down her white top with a hanky "Now, what can you tell me that you couldn't tell your dad or Uncle Mike?" she queried.

"Where's the Rookie?"

Connie didn't answer the question but rested her chin between her dimpled fingers.

"She's missing love, up near Devil's Rock. They've found her car, another unidentified car, ID and a Taser. We don't know if it is linked to you, "said Connie who wasn't one to sugar coat anything, ever. "We'll get back to her, but answer my questions first."

Gina took a small sip of tea and pulled a face. "It tastes like shit."

"Don't mince your words, darling child," Connie chuckled, it would take more than a kidnapper to break Gina's attitude.

"Ok, I'll talk but only if we can do my hair and face later," she raised her eyebrows, but the action hurt her head, she kind of ducked away from the pain. She continued, "So, I never saw his face, otherwise I would be dead right? He showed me pictures he took of me while I was unconscious. Dad can't ever see them if they come out in the investigation right? He also showed me photos of my early modelling days, pretty graphic Connie." Gina looked down into her lap wringing her hands together. She hated this stark white bedding, the feel of it too.

"Where did he source the photos?" She wrote something in her diary, although in a text only she could decipher.

"I presume the internet? Not sure really. They could be in anyone's hands. I can just picture them in a cheap dirty tabloid "'Police chief's daughter isn't so prim.'" She pouted at Connie.

"The truth madam, now," she had known her so long she knew when Gina was trying to manipulate a situation or wriggle out of something.

Gina jutted out her chin in defiance challenging Connie.

"I'm the victim here, Aunty Connie," she protested too much. "Shit, the only person who had some of those pictures was my boyfriend. I don't know how the kidnapper got them," she shivered.

Connie passed over a spare cardigan she had brought with her. Connie pondered the information Gina had just gave her before changing direction, although she noted 'BOYFRIEND' in her diary. She would get a colleague to look into it, or herself, it was about time she came off the front desk.

"What about him, your kidnapper and surroundings?' Connie took a gulp of her equally bad stewed tea.

"He had like a stuffy accent, you know posh. He said he had a plan and I wasn't his type." Connie raised her brows at Gina. "That's a first Aunty Con," she added playfully. "The room was something else though. I think Tess would need to hear about it pronto, it's her thing." Connie nodded and called Tess's number putting the phone on speaker. Tess answered immediately.

"Hey Tess, it's Connie, I'm with Gina, and yes she will be fine," Connie was pre-empting Tess's questions as she thought Tess needed to hear this right away.

"Hey Gina, go on Sweety," Tess said gently.

Gina cleared her throat then began to describe the room she had been kept in.

"There were like hundreds maybe thousands of skeletons, but like art, like an artist would do or sculptor had decorated their room with bones, not just stacked up. Under different circumstances I suppose they would've been beautiful in their own creepy way. I kind of got the feeling he was threatening me with the same outcome." Fucking creep she thought.

"Like the Sedlec Ossuary?" chimed in David 'Oh, sorry I'm Tess's colleague. Amazing really." Connie wasn't sure if he meant the Ossuary or being Tess's colleague.

"Boss, Dr MacLean, he's, my boss. In context this isn't too weird guys, think about it skeletons, used to be buried under the church floor before the reformation, anthropologically many communities like to have a link to their dead ancestors. In Rome there are churches decorated with human bones, it's not always as macabre as you think. Interesting though, as you would need lots of space and privacy. Mostly these things are a tourist destination or an attraction, so this is someone's private collection." This was really informative information that Gina had given. Patrick would need to know this ASAP. Tess was utterly intrigued.

They ended the call, Connie spoke to Patrick and Mike, relaying all the details Gina had given, even the photos, right now Gina's modesty was not on his priority list, but the boyfriend fucking was. Mike pointed out to Patrick that he was better going to question Gina's boyfriend and not him, the last thing they needed was Patrick in a cell for knocking the shit out of the little bastard. Patrick reluctantly agreed, he would concentrate his efforts finding the Rookie. Fuck knows what had happened to her. First thing you always do is let a colleague or family member know where you are going if you are a lone worker. The Rookie new that she was smart, so why? He wasn't driving, a helicopter had been scheduled to land, pick him up and take him to the search area. A police woman drove him to a nearby playing field where the helicopter could land. Patrick ducked instinctively as the craft whirred down noisily, the trees straining and moaning under the strain of the false wind. A beautiful sweet smell drafted from some sort of white flowering tree, the smell reminded him of Tess, the sweet but strong perfume she wore. This all started with Tess, everything was leading back to her original kidnap. He boarded the helicopter, strapped himself in, put on his earphones and introduced himself to the pilot. They exchanged pleasantries then up and off they went, the trees regaining some composure as they went, like a fallen boxer getting back to his feet.

Mike knocked a quick sharp wrap on The Boyfriend's door. Mike didn't have the patience for the little prick "Police, open up now," he bellowed through the letter box. He had an intimidating presence, so he had been told. The boyfriend opened the door and almost recoiled in fear. Mike pushed past him while flashing his ID.

"I suggest you sit down," Mike glowered down at him. The boyfriend was gym ripped, maybe a few steroids, but it was all for posing not fighting. "You know it's harder to punch someone when you are sitting down, SO FUCKING SIT!" Spittle flew out of his mouth hitting the boyfriends face as he shouted. The boyfriend sat down fast. Mike took in his surroundings, not a bad pad for a lad this age. Some fancy paint on the walls was coloured grey, huge sliding glass doors opened up to an impressive kitchen, most likely never used.

"How do you make your living," he asked glaring at the lad.

"You know I do new tube vids and I develop gaming, I'm a vlogger," he replied. The little shit looked a bit more comfortable now, a little cock sure of himself.

"A fucking what? You stupid twat!" Mike took out his packet of cigarettes and lit one, blowing smoke in the lads direction.

'Hey, you can't do that in here, it's disgusting." Although he protested he fetched a saucer from the kitchen and plonked it next to Mike.

"Yup," agreed Mike, it was a disgusting habit. Mike nodded to the fancy glass coffee table, a little white powder still present from the lad's last snort. "So is that. You want to start explaining why you have traces of coke on your coffee table? Or do we skip that and talk about the pictures of Gina?" He stamped his cigarette out angrily.

"I don't get the difference, Gina's a model anyhow. She's done worse than the photos I sold," he replied and as soon as he did so the lad realised his mistake as soon as it came out of his stupid veneered-toothed mouth. "Could I have a cigarette please?" he whined. Mike threw him a cig and the lighter. The lad lit but coughed loudly, it wasn't his drug of choice.

"After she vanished I got a call, was asked if I had any adult pictures of Gina, was offered really good money no questions asked though. The caller said the pictures would go to the highest bidder and they would sell for a fortune due to her disappearance. So I sold for 20k, didn't want to wait around, the guy transferred the money as soon as I dropped off the pictures." He looked guiltily at Mike.

"Why, why the fuck would you sell intimate pictures of someone you love, and what do you mean dropped them off?'

Mike stood up and slammed his fist into the trendy couch next to where the lad sat. The lad jumped and went white. He put his hands out in a-calm-down gesture, Mike just glowered at him.

"I was instructed to print off the pictures, glue them in a book that he instructed me to buy, something weird about standing stones. I don't know. I then had to drop the book off at an old weird bookstore with a freaky looking girl at the counter, left it for a Mr Henge to pick up. Me and Gina were just hooking up, kind of casual you know?" He put his head in his hands and started to cry, Mike was already out of the door as the lad looked up.

The helicopter landed in a field near an array of police vehicles, lights left on flashing and whirring. They were like a blot on the dark landscape. The pilot spoke to Patrick; they were scheduled to take up the copter to search once Patrick had an update. Patrick strode towards some officers that were stood heads together in serious chat; a forensic officer was sealing off the cars and dropped stun gun. Patrick motioned for them to gather round.

"Where's my fucking Rookie?"

Patrick got an instant feeling this wasn't related to Tess or the skeleton, something else, call it a 6th sense. An owl hooted and swooped for its prey; Patrick hoped it wasn't an omen. Some officers looked at each other, unsure if they should speak, a female officer stood forward leading the group.

"Sir, I'm PC Hodges, I'll give you an update," she said as she held out her hand, gripped Patrick's hand in a firm shake. She was petite and rotund. Heifer Hodges they had called her at school, including two of the male officers stood here tonight, who both glanced at one another and smirked. Patrick caught them, he also saw PC Hodges discomfort but ultimately her courage. He smiled at her.

"Something funny boys> Cos I don't see anything fucking funny about tonight, so fucking share your joke," he demanded. His

Glaswegian voice was quiet, menacing in fact. The two men shook their heads not daring to speak, they were from another police station but they had all heard about Patrick, his reputation. The Wee Yin they nicknamed him, it was a bit of a joke as Patrick was built like an ox but no one had ever called him it to his face. Patrick took PC Hodges aside so he could concentrate on what she was saying, he asked the forensic guy to join them. The forensic guy was an older man named Jo, his grey beard framed his warm face, his white hair like a mad professors.

"If I may, Sir?" PC Hodges asked. Patrick nodded eagerly.

"I put a trace on her phone, a few texts and calls to her dad, then she receives a call from an unknown caller, tracked her phone to this location then nothing. Her shift had technically ended but Connie said the Rookie had said she was staying, just popping out for lunch then coming back and working through the night, her dad clarifies this too. I've called all the take-aways to see if they remember her getting something to eat but nothing, unless she went to the 24-hour supermarket which I haven't checked yet. One car belongs to the Rookie and the other we don't know but it's a crap old car."

Patrick looked up in thought then nodded to forensic Jo.

"Well guys this is a strange one, the Taser is police issue." Jo looked to Patrick who was already on his phone his face and angry shade of red.

Tess 2006

Tess was trying to work out how to appease the angry young man who stood in her way. She stifled tears that wanted to break free and show her weakness. The walls of the dank dark toilets seemed to be crushing her. She had an overwhelming feeling of claustrophobia. Again her tormentor leant down to her, intimidating her with his height, she could see yellow headed spots on his face and neck. It made her feel sick.

"A young girl should be very careful what she wishes from an older boy," he hissed in her ear then licked her neck. She recoiled in horror, the bile rising in her throat. Then she grabbed his crotch, she twisted, dug in her long elegant nails, and he let out the most satisfying screech she had ever heard. She pushed him away just as the Eminem look-a-like Dylan rushed into the loos.

"Hey, Ricky, fuck sake man, leave her alone. She's just a kid," he said as he punched Ricky's arm.

Tess saw it as her chance to get away and hurried out of that horrible toilet. She threw Dylan a disgusted look. She re-joined her friends, who were oblivious to the danger she had just encountered, danced on happily and noisily. Tess wasn't sure she wanted to grow up, it seemed like a minefield. Little did she know that next summer her minefield would turn nuclear.

The Bookshop

Mike had called the owners and their daughter insisting they meet him at their bookstore. He arrived and knocked hard on the door. An older arty looking lady answered the door dressed in dungarees, her hair dishevelled, glasses perching on top of it trying to contain the abundance of grey curls. She let Mike in with a curt nod and led him to a table at the back of the shop where her husband and daughter sat drinking green tea. They offered some to Mike but he declined. He had already described what had happened over the phone so they had some idea of why they were here. The daughter had lots of piercings and tattoos, her hair a weird shade of public toilet blue. A fan in the corner whizzed trying to cool the hot night air, it failed miserably. Mike placed his large hands on the table.
"Who is he?" he enquired losing patience.

The mother and daughter looked at each other, as they did Mike could see the resemblance, both had a mole, or beauty spot on her face just under her nose, their features were delicate and feminine, though the daughter seemed to be fighting this, like it was a curse. The piercings and tattoos made her seem harsh, but too forced, like a defence barrier, a man-made sea defence where the rocks are too perfectly placed but when challenged by the roaring force of the sea no damage is done, the defence deflects harm. She was about to speak but the father held out his hands in a cut-off motion, silencing both mother and daughter.

"Please, please?" he begged, then put his head in his hands and started to sob. "I'll talk, just spare them the pain." The man looked up at Mike his face an ashen shade, imploring Mike with his eyes. The daughter stood and kissed the top of her dad's head, as did her mother, as they left the room the mother gave a small smile to

Mike, and then vanished up a narrow spiral staircase crying as she went.

Mike pulled out a chair, it was painted a sage green probably posh paint, with pink roses painted on its frame, he felt as stupid as he most likely looked. His long legs found it difficult to find any space under the cramped table. He made himself as comfy as a giant in a school chair then nodded for the man, Andrew to carry on. Andrew sipped at his green Chinese tea, wiped his mouth with his hanky then spoke.

"I was only about 25, found myself a job at a stately home in Scotland. You know nothing much just a labourer, handyman, gardener, whatever. A nice little cottage thrown into the employment deal. The cottage was ramshackle with no central heating but I didn't care, I was independent," he lit a cigarette as he spoke and offered Mike one, Mike took one, lit it and inhaled.

"The boss was a dick, you know, wealthy, up his own arse. His brother was a politician. Both born with silver spoons. Anyhow, their sister Dina, now my wife was something else completely. She was arty and hippy like, stunningly beautiful, tall blond just like her mother I suppose. Dina had a little girl." He motioned his head towards upstairs. "That's them, the absolute loves of my life. I would do anything for them. I did actually." He took another long drag of his cig feeling the hit as it made him lightheaded. From the stairway where she disappeared reappeared Dina, she walked over to the table and scooped up the cigarettes in her hand. Mike thought she was going to scold Andrew, but she walked away with them in her grasp, looked over her shoulder as if reading Mikes mind and said, "I think both Hazel and I need a nicotine hit." With that she vanished up the magic staircase again. Andrew stubbed out is cigarette then carried on with his story.

"I had fallen in love with Dina, then one day she just went! I was devastated even though I wasn't sure she felt the same. Dina took Mimmy with her but then Mimmy came back. Mimmy and I grew close, like a father and daughter. I could see she was unhappy and she would confide in me. She hated her uncle the boss, she was only little but she had the courage to hand me her mum's phone number; she was gutsy like her mum. I called Dina, and secretly visited her. We fell in love and she told me the whole disgusting story. Hazel is the result of her brother raping her, Dina over and over again all her life. He took out a hanky and wiped his eyes, blew his nose. Dina looked just like her mother, she was an anthropologist. Motherhood never did it for her so she left the husband and kids in search of excitement. Ended up in Egypt as a Doctor. She died in a car accident years ago. Anyhow Laird was left with his two twin boys and Dina, when he died the boys were old enough to take responsibility of Dina, one went off to become a successful politician the other was awkward with a cruel streak."

The family had mainly hid him from public view, he was obsessed with his mother and also her looks, of course Dina inherited her mother's looks. She got pregnant with Mimmy and tried to leave many times but he always dragged her back. This time he only brought back Mimmy. Dina was beside herself with loss. Initially I wanted to kill him, if I'm brutally honest. Then we decided to focus on his greed. Dina contacted him asking for access to Mimmy which on occasions when it suited him he gave. She was working as a teacher at that point. We confronted him and told him she would walk away with Mimmy for a paltry 100k, just enough to start a business and deposit for our house, in return she would sign over her share of the vast family fortunes, and I mean vast. If you include assets, property, land, rivers, art, jewellery as well as cash then you are talking about 200 million."

Mike blew out his cheeks. Dina seemed like such a normal woman really. Dina then continued, "He agreed which we didn't expect without a fight, he looked gleeful. I remember just wanting to punch his lights out. He suggested we buy this book shop, that he worked with MI6 and occasionally he would need to drop off a book for someone else to pick up. We had heard rumours he had links to the secret service so we reluctantly agreed. Very occasionally he would visit, no one could stand him and Mimmy had now been told the truth; that he was really her biological father and uncle."

Dina and Mimmy entered the room hand in hand, Hazel ran over to her step-father and hugged him tightly, he hugged her back both cried. Dina looked at them both a small sad smile appearing on her face, she took over.

"A young man left a book for him a few weeks ago, we had always been told never to look inside the books and we didn't. We just wanted to get on with our lives. I was and am scared of my brother. I always will be to some extent." She didn't need to explain anymore, it was obvious how much power her brother yielded.

"What about your other brother?" asked Mike.

"He's not too nice either. He hides behind his political status but he is awful. He tends to keep his distance though which is fine by me. So there you have it, an incestuous lot. Though my father was a good man, I like to think Mimmy and I share his genes." She smiled again at Mimmy.

Mike offered everyone a cigarette, they all took one and lit up. He gave them a moment to digest not only the nicotine but why he was possibly there.

"There's a link between the man that left the book, it had indecent images of a policeman's daughter that had been kidnapped. The man sold the images to your fucking brother. She has a link to an archaeologist who was kidnapped as a teenager, who is also the policeman's girlfriend." Mike let that sink in. Andrew, Dina and Mimmy looked at one another astounded. Dina was now much more animated.

"I can show you my family estate if you want? Well it's not mine anymore. The thing is I know every nook and cranny so if he's hiding something I will find it."

Mike did a curt nod then said "Come on, let's go." They all grabbed a few belongings then followed Mike out of the door.

From The Disco To The Depths

David had nipped out to get some fresh good coffee from the local café and morning rolls, Tess stepped out to make a call to her regression therapist, she needed to see her today. Her therapist answered quickly, she could see her but it would have to be ASAP. Tess texted David to say hold the breakfast, she would be back in a few hours. As she unlocked her car her phone went.

"Hey, Tess here." She sat in the driver's seat, keys in the ignition.

"Sorry to bother you Tess, Its Dylan, I wondered if we could meet up in person."

She let out a puff of air. "Gosh Dylan, I am pretty snowed under at the moment, could you not just speak over the phone?" She really was in a hurry today. She turned the ignition.

"Tess, I will be quick, my car is parked behind yours. I hope you don't mind the intrusion? I really need to talk about stuff." He knocked on her car window.

Tess jumped; she hadn't expected him to be here. For fuck sake.

"Five minutes she mouthed to him while showing him five finger digits. She got out of her car, not locking it this wouldn't take long. She followed Dylan to his car and got in the passenger seat, he started to drive off.

"Dylan, I haven't got time for a merry-go-round, where are we going?"

"Sorry," he replied but there was something in his voice. Tess felt her head being restrained then something over her mouth and nose, she kicked out fighting, fighting as she had always done, the darkness started to engulf her body and mind, she hadn't any fight left in her, she let it take her to that dark, dark place.

Dylan drove carefully, the man in the car behind following him. He drove five minutes to an underpass. The underpass entered a derelict yard, nothing here, no cameras, or witnesses. The large man got out of his car. It looked like some sort of government car, big black and fancy. He opened Tess's side and lifted her out of the car, then gently placing her in the boot. Dylan was relieved the man was so gentle with Tess. The man strode over to Dylan, he had a vicious scar on his cheek, ragged and ugly, he opened his phone and showed Dylan images, filthy vile disgusting images of girls his own kids ages, filth that somehow had made its way onto Dylan's computer. Dylan felt bad for Tess but he had to do this to save himself and his family. He was sorry.

"You utter one word and your life is over. Your kids will go into care, you to jail as a nonce, and your wife, well she will go off with her lover, she might do that anyway." He punched Dylan once in the liver. Dylan Fell to his knees, retching in agony but nothing came out just spit. The man then rained more blows down on Dylan. Still on all fours he looked up and the car, driver and contents were gone. The derelict buildings seemed as dirty as those images, dark and filthy. Dylan sobbed.

The Rookie

He had started to climb upwards towards her. Her hand throbbed in pain from the agonising break. She had tried to summon the strength to climb but with her broken hand it was impossible, she would fall. She needed two hands to grasp the protruding ledge that was the devils forehead. Even in daylight, without any breaks and with hydration she would struggle to make that climb, instead she sat there, startled, waiting her demise.

"Do you know the worst of it bitch, eh? If you could've just taken some banter and not been so frigid we would still be working together on that missing bitch's case. You fucking women now-a-days just can't toe the line can you?"

He went to reach another hole with his hand but it slipped, some rocks scuttled down the steep surface reminding him of the height and danger of this climb. This time he found and gripped the hole, then another, pushing himself up with his feet, his strength was far superior to hers. He was made for fighting, a warrior, her for making babies and cooking.

She could've sworn she had heard a helicopter in the distance, YES! Yes, she could see its lights searching desperately for her in the dark.

"It's over," she shouted down to him, "just stop and give yourself up'. Her relief was short-lived as that seemed to motivate and spur him on. The Rookie noticed the weather changing, the air seemed thick and close.

The Cop reached for the next ledge or hole where he could place his hand, the weather had changed though and the moonlight no longer lit his way, thick fog had descended onto the devils gorge, he couldn't see his hand a few inches away from him. Never mind, he would just use his sense of touch more, he felt for another ledge for his right hand to cling to, he felt along jagged rock face but finally found another hold, he would have to stretch as far as his body would let him, like a criminal attached to a medieval torture rack, his body protesting in pain. Yet no matter how bad the pain he had to make her pay, make her pay for destroying his life.

The Girlfriend

Everything had come as such a shock to her, although it shouldn't have on reflection of his toxicity. From the moment they met he had controlled her, he professed to doing it out of love and concern for her but now she was certain he was just a narcissist or worse. They had met online his profile seemed to match hers perfectly, now she wondered if he had conjured that up to match hers, it was creepy.

She unlocked the door to their flat, aware that, that was pretty stupid, to be here alone. She glanced at her reflection in the hallway mirror, the bruising to her cheek now subsiding, it's a shame the emotional trauma didn't fade like the bruises. The wallpaper, mirror and lighting all his choice of style, in fact he chose it all, made all of the decisions from what clothing she did or didn't wear to the bed they shared. God, she had loved him fiercely, despite her family and friends highlighting red flags. She headed for the living room, went straight for the drinks cabinet and poured herself a large vodka and tonic, something he wouldn't allow her to drink as he said it was too masculine, normally she drank prosecco or G & T. It felt liberating drinking what she wanted, her choice. With that she looked at her clothing, all drab hiding her femininity something before she had met him she embraced. She wore a long shapeless black skirt, a boring plain t-shirt and t-shirt bra so men wouldn't see her underwear. She headed upstairs to their shared dressing room and paused at the bedroom door. She inhaled her breath sharply, recalling the numerous times he had raped her on that bed. All the time telling her she was fat, useless and worthless. She should count herself lucky he wanted her. So she did just that, counted herself lucky he had chosen to be with her when, like he said he could've settled down with a really beautiful woman.

Now she was furious, she dragged the sheets, pillow and duvet into a bundle opened the bedroom window and threw them out onto the lawn. There was something really satisfying seeing them sprawled on the lawn all dirty, this was so cleansing. Next she went to the dressing room, she looked through rows and rows of her old clothes, they had tags he had put on them such as too fat, too slutty, asking for it, slag! She wasn't allowed to wear these ever. She pulled out a stunning red halter-neck dress. She tore off her clothing, all of it, and searched in her underwear drawer. Again labelled, too ugly for red, too boring for black, too plain for pastels, each in their own drawer. The bottom drawer was labelled 'allowed'. In this drawer was the drabbest underwear you would ever see. Off white garments that didn't enhance her figure, big knickers that had no shape, she tore off the label then proceeded to throw them out of the same bedroom window not caring who saw her naked.

She returned to the dressing room, boring grey wallpaper adorned the walls like a dreary state school toilet block, it gave the impression of some formidable teacher daring you to challenge all things bleak, daring to express yourself. She took out some beautiful delicate red French underwear she had purchased on a visit to Paris; she put them on and turned to look in the full length mirror attached to the door, many doors of her prison she thought. She was taken back, her reflection was stunning. She was beautiful. Her long red hair cascaded over her shoulder. She wasn't an ugly Ginner as he had called her but a vibrant red head, with bold green eyes she was unique not ugly. Her breasts and bottom voluptuous but her stomach flat, her legs long and toned, a few stretch marks indicated her history with dieting. She would never diet again! She threw on the red dress and it hugged her curves like a racing driver hugged the sharpness of a bend. She was simply stunning. She smiled at her reflection something she had not done in three years.

She headed down to the living room and noticed the corner of something poking out from under the boring grey couch. She bent down and retrieved it. A laptop, one she had not seen before. Slightly confused she sat on the couch reaching for her drink to give her courage to look at the laptop. She caressed the computer like it was a valuable prize, not yet daring to open it up, scared of what it might reveal.

The internet hadn't been switched off, which she found odd as he was even controlling about energy use, maybe he was in a rush? She flipped open the laptop, switched it on and a screen challenged her to enter a password. Police1 she entered, he had that for a few of his passwords, like he was the top policeman. 'Not recognised' the screen screamed at her. OK, SIMLPY THE BEST she typed, his favourite song, he would sing it to himself, the irony that Tina Turner had been the victim of horrific domestic violence was lost, or was it? DENIED! THIS DEVICE WILL BE LOCKED AFTER ONE MORE TRY! The screen seemed to relay this information angrily. She thought and thought of him, his personality, and their relationship. 'STUPIDFATCUNT' she almost laughed and cried as she typed. The computer whirred into action and said welcome master! Of course this is how he referred to her! Imagine that 20 or so times a day. That's how she felt until now. Not so fucking stupid after all she said to herself smiling at the laptop.

She looked up his search history. She then clicked on each search. He wasn't even clever enough to delete or go into incognito.

'How to get away with murder'
'Concealing evidence'
'Sexual harassment in the workplace'
'Protected characteristics, employment law UK'
'Using a Taser to incapacitate'

'Rape porn'
'Child porn'

Of all of them the last one sucked the breath right out of her body, she gagged, the vodka wanted to vomit from her body. She ran to the kitchen sink and the vodka got its wish. She gagged again and again. When the feeling of nausea passed she still stood over the sink wondering if her mouth would start to erupt again. After a while she ran herself a glass of water drinking slowly, and then she returned to his laptop.

She couldn't even bring herself to view the horrors in his search history; instead she went to his pictures. 'Pictures of the Rookie.' She clicked on the title, she was apprehensive but courageous. His suspension due to his behaviour towards his young colleague had brought about the demise of their relationship. She had finally understood what her family and friends had been saying all along, that he was a predator and narcissist. Little did they know he was also a rapist and perpetrator of domestic violence.

The photos had started innocently, the rookie smiling as she started her journey as a rookie police officer. They eventually became more sinister. She viewed photos he had taken that were invasive without the Rookie's knowledge. Each had a label. 'Bitch is broken.' The rookie was crying, the photo was intrusive, a private moment he had chosen to invade. 'Fucking lesbo.' Photos of her rumoured lover, taken or stolen from social media, the girls enjoying Ghyll scrambling. 'Up-skirt.' Taken on a night out, her unaware he had crossed professional and all legal boundaries taking a photo of her in a drunken state, pointing the camera up her skirt as she got into a taxi.

'Nearly ☺.' The Rookie stripped down to her underwear. OMFG with a winking emoji. Putting the Rookie to bed on the same night out. How fucking sick is he? 'Wish list.' She held down more puke! This one was the vilest thing she had ever seen in her life. This was a video, modified by putting the Rookies face on disgusting hard porn images of a women being subjected to rape, then murder! Snuff porn or something it was called.

'End result.' A picture of the Rookie superimposed onto either a dead woman or a staged dead woman. Superimposed onto the dead emaciated body of a starving woman posed in a sexually suggestive manner! She gagged again, but held it down. She would not allow herself to be controlled by fear, her body or another human being ever again. She retrieved her handbag and dialled 999 knowing the possibilities of that action, fully aware an officer who shared the same sick values as her ex-boyfriend might attend her call. She had her dongle with her, she always had it due to her work in HR,. She transferred everything to her dongle for her own safety.

The Search

Patrick ducked under the whirring blades of the helicopter then hopped in the front seat next to the pilot. He put on earphones so they could communicate.

"Hello sir' said the pilot," they knew each other so didn't need further introductions. "Weather forecast isn't great so we have to move."

Patrick nodded, affirming the need to proceed urgently. The blades of the helicopter whirred faster and faster until the helicopter lifted from the ground then hovered momentarily like a Hummingbird unsure whether to fly forwards or backwards. Patrick took in the landscape; he could see the two parked cars beneath him, then a river and gorge in the distance. He could see his home-land way out in the distance, calling him home. Soon, in a blink fog descended from his land over the border like King Malcolm III invading England in a cloak of war that would take them to Alnwick. Both he and the pilot had on headphones so they could communicate. Both were concerned about the distant fog.

Shit, Patrick thought, just as he spotted two people low beneath them, one possibly the Rookie was crouched on a ledge higher than the second person, the second person threw objects at the Rookie. It was The Cop. He momentarily stopped to look in their direction as did the Rookie who waved her arms frantically. The fog was rolling quickly towards them. the pilot turned to Patrick and shook his head.

"Five Minutes?' Patrick questioned The pilot re-iterated 5 with his fingers. They hovered lower now; the search light highlighted the people even more. Patrick spoke through a speaker.

"It's over! Give yourself up," he bellowed into the microphone, with that the pilot made a chopping motion with his hand signalling that was it time had ran out. The helicopter jerked upwards leaving the distressed Rookie and her pursuer.

Is This Really The End?

The Rookie's heart sank as she watched the helicopter jerk upwards quickly and head away from them. The only thing was they had a definite location now, but the difficulty would be the weather and terrain. Still watching the helicopter she tried to think of her next move as the cop was gaining ground. She heard a noise as loud as thunder but creaking.

"No," she shouted as the helicopter crashed in the distance. It had spiralled down and down all the time making a groaning noise it looked like a giant fly plummeting to its death. Then the loud bang as it hit the earth. The Rookie sobbed out loud.

"Oh, boo hoo," mocked the cop from below "Who's going to save you now?" He laughed as he carried on upwards towards her

So close now she could almost smell his rancid breath and cheap aftershave. She couldn't stay on this ledge and she couldn't climb over the ridge with her fucked up hand. The only way she could go was down. How on earth she would be able to swim though was another thing. She had the element of surprise on her side plus the fog was moving in fast. As quick as a falcon diving for its prey she launched herself off of the ledge, she had pushed herself forward like a spring remembering the jagged rocks jutting out from the pool close to the rock face. She hit the cold water fast, crying with pain as her hand hit the surface she gulped in some water. She went deep under, resisting the urge to cough for that would make her take in more water and risk drowning. Her chest hurt as she expelled air from her lungs. The natural urge to breathe engulfed her. As soon as she could she turned in the direction of the surface, not having any idea where the cop was. She could only guess he would follow her in or make for his escape climbing over the ridge.

The cold water had actually calmed down the pain in her hand, numbing it slightly. She was relieved of that. She swam as fast as she could down river, this was much easier than going against the flow of the water. When she felt herself tiring she turned onto her back and let the current do the work. The fog was clearing, she could see stars in the sky and hoped Patrick would live to see the sky again. Tears fell from her eyes. She cried so much that her salty tears could have turned the fresh water into an ocean. She looked at the rock face but the cop was nowhere in sight. If he had followed her he would be closing in real soon. As strong a swimmer as she was, she was no match for the strength of a man especially with her injury. It was scary not knowing if your pursuer was going to suddenly grab your leg and pull you under. The trees by the riverbank looked eerie in the darkness. She had a feeling that she was being watched. She would rather be in the water than pushing through thick vegetation that lined the ground, brambles and thick ferns. She ploughed on.

The cop hadn't expected her to dive back into the murky river. He had to make his decision quickly. Did he chase her? I mean he hated the bitch but that would be playing into the other cops hands. He would maybe catch her and could drown her. She couldn't swim fast or fight with her smashed hand. But wasn't that cutting off his nose to spite his face? He could make the difficult climb over the ridge, hike back into town to his girlfriend's. He controlled her so much she would hide him no problem. His uncle had a boat he could get to that then head for Ireland maybe. Yes, that was what he was going to do. He was such a talented climber, most wouldn't challenge the ridge but he had free climbed a lot. He started his ascent, carefully finding foot and hand holes, he pulled himself up slowly, it wasn't as easy as he had envisaged, the ridge jutted out sharply, hence the name of the devils brow. He moved one hand over the ridge looking for holes or something he could grip, once he had found two good hand grips he would just pull himself over the ridge. Lucky he had good upper body strength. Gripping tightly to the first hand hole he soon found the second. It felt like a sharp bit of rock. He smiled inwardly to himself, fuck he was good. He took a deep breath then heaved himself upwards using only his hands. That's it, nearly there; he smiled again cock sure as usual. The same time that he heard the crack was the exact time he fell. The rock hadn't been strong enough to take his body weight. He screamed as he went cursing The Rookie too. His head partly hit the rocks below first, but he was still conscious. He was conscious when his body unhooked from the rocks and started to join the rivers current. He was conscious when he started to go under slowly. He was conscious when he gagged on water. He was conscious as he started to panic. He was conscious when his leg snagged something underneath the murky water. He was conscious when his foot became entangled in that something. He was conscious when The Rookie spotted him. He was conscious when The Rookie thought about helping him. He was conscious when she turned her back and swam on. He was unconscious soon after.

Lost Dog

Tess was dreaming. In the dream she ran after her dog calling out his name desperately. The sky was blue not a cloud in sight, her long blond hair flowing behind her. She had had a note from Dylan, he had asked her to meet up here, said to destroy the note as he would be embarrassed if anyone found out due to their age-gap.

"Hey." Startled she turned round to see Dylan.

"I've lost my dog," she cried, wiping her eyes on her forearm. She was so upset she didn't even notice Dylan had grown the bleach out of his hair or was wearing a hoodie in this heat. He held out a bunch of flowers for her.

"Smell them, they're beautiful." He seemed a little nervous.

"I don't have time. I want my dog." She looked at him confused.

"Please Tess, the scent will wear off." He held them up to her nose.

She did as he had asked and breathed in deeply. The flowers smelt, smelt like . . . she had trouble focusing, everything was going dark. Dylan caught her as she fell.

"Tess, wake up Tess." Dylan roughly shook her shoulders, she opened her eyes. Terror enveloped her entire being. It wasn't Dylan, it was him, older, but him. Her mouth was parched. He looked round at her surroundings. The room was unlit and old, a huge skeleton chandelier hung from the grand ceiling, other bones decorated the ceiling. Human bones. That was not what scared her, as an archaeologist she had seen this numerous times in her career, under different circumstances it would be fascinating. Him though, he scared her to death. He had ruined her life. She had been suffering since she was just 13 years old. Something sparked in her mind, Dylan. She was confused, previously she had a memory that when she was kidnapped someone grabbed her from behind and held something over her nose and mouth. Or was that her mind playing tricks? Maybe the dawning of the truth would be too traumatic. She hadn't been dreaming just then, but remembering. How had she got from being with Dylan? Why had Dylan sparked such a memory? How had she gone from chatting to Dylan to being kidnapped by this man?

David

David turned his car into the lab car park, he had read Tess's text message that she was seeing her therapist, something he encouraged regardless of the pressure they were under. Oh, she was back already, her car was parked up albeit oddly. He went into the lab stuck his belongings into his locker then changed into sterile overalls. "Hey Tess how's it going? he asked. She wasn't there. He checked the staff room, nothing.

He asked the security desk if they had seen her. The security man looked confused. He shook his chubby head. "She went out earlier but I presumed she was still out as her cars not on camera, the camera doesn't extend all the way back. Unless she came in when I was on my lunch." He bent down to double check his camera, again shaking his head.

"Ok, thanks," replied. He was growing concerned now as she was nowhere in that building. He headed out to her car, he peered inside the window, her bag and phone lay on the passenger seat. 'FUCK, FUCK' He ran back inside the lab shouting for the security guy to call the police. He ran and retrieved his own phone from his locker. He had put Patrick's number in his phone for work purposes. He unlocked the screen scrolled to contacts and called Patrick, nothing, no answer.

Gina was in the middle of moving her things into her new flat. Her dad and Tess deserved a little privacy she thought. Gina's phone rang. It was the police station, most likely her dad with an update.

"Hey dad, what's up?" she smiled as she asked. 'WHAT, OH NO! NO! NO!" She raced from the flat to her car, a little mini convertible that could move. Traffic beeped as she weaved in between cars and flew through red lights. The town was soon a backdrop as she sped through little country lanes, hills and castles in the distance she was on the scene in 45 minutes. Police car upon police car, fire engine upon fire engine, and mountain rescue team all near the scene. They had all congregated where the two cars had originally been found, the terrain too rugged for vehicles other than 4 x 4's. Gina hurried from her car towards a police car and ambulance. A girl younger than her sat with a heat blanket draped over her shoulders. A paramedic was administering first aid and drip fed pain-killers. As Gina got closer she recognised the girl from school, it was The Rookie, brilliant talent her dad had told her. The Rookie had tears streaming down her face, Gina got the feeling the tears weren't for herself but someone else.

Gina fell to her knees, hands in prayer "NO, OH MY GOD DAD, DAD!" she yelled. A paramedic ran over to console her. He led her over to the ambulance, gently sitting her down next to The Rookie. Gina could smell burning and fuel, she gagged then threw up on the grass below. The Rookie put her arms around Gina and hugged her tightly.

"It's my fault, all my fault, if he hadn't suspended him this would never have happened. I'm so, so sorry, Gina."

Gina buried her head in The Rookie's arms sobbing loudly. Gina looked at The Rookie, "The only person at fault is that nasty bastard. I hope he dies." The Rookie replied, "Dead.". In that moment they knew that only each other would know what that statement meant. Gina nodded slowly taking it in. PC Hodges approached them both, she looked ashen.

"Search and rescue are out there. We're doing everything we can."

She bent down and gently kissed each woman on the side of the face. At that moment The Rookie's dad emerged at the scene. He ran towards The Rookie as fast as he could and scooped her up like a child. Finally she felt. Totally safe. She only ever did in his arms. Gina watched them both sobbing quietly, not wanting to ruin their joy but aware that she might never get this moment with her dad.

Back in Glasgow Jinty checked her phone; she had texted Tess hours ago but no reply. Usually no matter how busy her schedule Tess would text back. Jinty hit Tess's contact. She relaxed as the phone dial ended and Tess picked up.

"Thank God, Tess. I was worried sick," she sighed while lighting a fag.

"It's her colleague, David. Is this Jinty?"

"Yes," she answered confused, shushing her kids who sounded like feral animals.

"She's missing, Jinty. The police are on their way. I'm trying to get hold of Patrick but nothing doing. Do you have his daughter's number?"

"Oh God, please let her be safe," she cried, putting herself on loud speaker she scrolled through her phone and found Gina's number. "I had a few of her contacts just in case this ever happened. I never thought it would." She gave David the number. He thanked her then promptly hung up.

He dialled Gina's number. Gina had the phone in her hand, somethings never change. The number wasn't one of her contacts. Under normal circumstances she wouldn't take a call from an unknown number, too many scammers and cold callers. These weren't normal circumstances.

"Hello," Gina's words came out in a sob.

"Hi, this is David, Tess's colleague, I take it you've heard then?" He sounded sombre.

"Heard what?" she asked confused, or maybe he was about to tell her about her dads crash.

David cleared his throat and gulped, "Tess is missing. That's all we know for now. I'm trying to get hold of your dad. I got your number from Jinty."

"OMFG," she mouthed, "David, dad has been in a helicopter crash, we have no idea if he survived. I thought this day couldn't get any worse. I'm going to contact Mike, he'll know what to do."

David thanked her, saying the usual *if there's anything I can do* speech, she was grateful.

She called Mike, both signals weren't great as he was already onto something and heading to Scotland. He eventually got the gist of what she was saying. The heat was on now to solve this; Tess's life was in imminent danger and Patrick, fucking hell, he dare not think.

The police had cordoned off Tess's car and possessions. It was getting late now, the heat turning from heavy to muggy bringing a strong pleasant scent in the air. David spoke with the investigators, asking for permission to go to the lab as they had unfinished business with the skeleton and the Cartier bracelet. The police officer in charge said he would escort David. The officer followed David down into the lab, David pulled out a drawer which contained numbered bags of evidence retrieved from the skeleton. He lay the contents of bag 10 out under a microscope, moving the bracelet so he could see the hallmark that would identify the maker, although they already knew it was Cartier. David took a note of the mark, he then gently put the bracelet back into the bag and into the drawer. He called Cartier London. A woman answered with a snooty voice, addressing herself as the manager.

"Hello," said David, "I am working on a police investigation and need to know if I can trace who bought this item through its hallmark please?" He glanced at the police officer for support, he nodded.

"I'm afraid we don't give out that information, sir. Our clients are some of the wealthiest in the world. Confidentiality is also our hallmark," she whispered to someone in the background.

The police officer beckoned for David to pass him the phone which he did. Officer Green cleared his throat before speaking, "Mam, I would suggest you co-operate with us as we have urgent police business to attend. We are investigating numerous possible murders and kidnappings. Now I can get a warrant but if someone hinted to the press what was going on I don't think that would be good for sales. AM I MAKING MYSELF CLEAR? He spelt that out slowly. Again he heard whispering in the background.

"Of course, of course we will help' she sounded worried, "but where possible could we prefer to keep other clients out of this'

Officer Green looked at David annoyance and anger etched on his face.

"Mam, your clients are the least of my worries, now talk."

After their conversation ended the officer called colleagues in London and requested that they interview all staff, seize records too just in case.

Officer Green turned to David who waited patiently, "The piece was originally commissioned for a renowned politician back in 2007. He paid approximately 12k for it." He smiled. "We now have a lead'. David smiled back, god he hoped they could save Tess.

Flapping Wings

Gina wouldn't budge from the search site, she simply couldn't. So she sat in her car waiting for news. The minutes seemed like an eternity. Dawn was breaking now and a lazy hazy sun was rising in a clear sky. The Rookie had gone in the ambulance, she would be ok, and her hand was fractured. She was starving and thirsty though and looked like some swamp monster. Her dad had followed the ambulance in his car. He had never been so relieved in his entire life. He kept thanking God, saying he would pray more. He most likely wouldn't. Tonight he and his daughter Rachel, even he called her Rookie now more often than not, would get a take-away have a movie night huddled together on the sofa. He dearly hoped Gina got the news that would make this a reality for her in the future.

Dylan drove home to his wife and kids fully aware that his actions both now and historically had caused the kidnap and God knows what else to Tess. He hadn't wanted any of this. His father Paul worked for the Artist as his minder and doing any dirty work the Artist needed taken care of. The Artist was the only person in the world that his father gave a shit about. He certainly didn't give a shit about him which is why he beat him up. He was evil. Pure evil. Even as a teenager Tess was brave and fought like hell, inflicting that scar on his father's face, biting him like a rabid dog. He had never in his life dared to stand up to him, not ever. When his parents had been married life had been hell. His dad was in the SAS, all he seemed to know was brutality.

When his father was deployed, life with his mother was wonderful. They had lived in Germany and Cyprus and would enjoy the company of locals and their culture. When he returned home he would rain terror and blows on them both. Finally his mother was brave enough to take the two of them and escape to a shelter. She did this when they were back visiting York in England. His hideous father had insisted on visiting rights. He didn't want to see Dylan really, just terrorise him and his mother. Having much more expendable cash, access to lawyers and the fact his mother had never reported the abuse to English police, Paul succeeded in the courts and received visiting rights. Anyhow, that night at the youth club, Paul had come to pick him and his friends up and had spotted Tess. He asked lots of questions about her and said he thought she looked familiar. Then Paul hatched his first plan. He said Dylan would have to lure Tess to him and that his boss had to have her. Dylan couldn't believe what he had been asked to do. Paul made it clear if he didn't carry out his orders he would kill his mother. Coerced Dylan reluctantly agreed to the plan. Both times. He turned into his drive, got out of his car and entered the ex-council house. His wife was in the modern airy living room. She let out a gasp when she saw him. He made his decision.

"Call the police."

Mike

Mike was a little hesitant boarding the police helicopter with Dina, Andy and Mimmy, for obvious reasons. But they needed to get to the estate on the West coast of Scotland quickly. Time wasn't on Tess's side. It would take them over an hour to get there, although the local Scottish police service had been informed of the urgency. Mike knew Dina, Andy and Mimmy were the only ones who really knew the estate well enough to find Tess. The scenery on the journey was stunning. They flew above rivers, hills, lakes, farms, forests, Munros and lochs. At any other time this would've been a dream flight, at this moment though Mike didn't know if his friend or Tess were alive. That thought was harrowing.

They started their descent, the pilot informing them of their imminent landing, they all held on tightly. The helicopter descended slowly, carefully. The police were already on the scene searching the estate, needle in a haystack as the place was huge. A castle stood proudly dominating a hill overlooking a beautiful Loch. However, scattered all over the estate were livestock sheds, outbuildings, workers cottages and stables. Mike thanked the pilot and raced from the helicopter. Dina, Andy and Mimmy followed on. Mike spoke to the detective in charge DCI Fellows who had worked with Patrick out of Glasgow a number of years ago. DCI Fellows had salt and pepper hair, was a little rotund and his suit was straining at the girth under the pressure.

DCI Fellows addressed the group, "Ok let's go, let's go." This time it was Dina who led the way, they all followed.

The Politician

Back in Leeds The Politician was leading a Tory party surgery. They were in a quaint village hall on the outskirts of Leeds, an expensive leafy area. He liked the sound of his own voice; he was a very pompous man. He was talking about public services pay rises and how they weren't possible. Two police officers sneaked in the back, they watched and listened to him for a few minutes. The female officer glanced at her male colleague and they both raised their eyebrows. They walked to the front of the crowd and got the Politician's attention. He looked sideways at them in annoyance. The female officer gave him a little dignity and whispered in his ear.

"I beg your pardon?'" He shook his head angrily. "Absolute nonsense. Now shoo."

The male officer stepped forward while reaching for his handcuffs, he grabbed the politician forced his hands behind his back and proceeded to cuff him.

"You are under arrest Sir, on suspicion of being involved in the kidnapping of Teresa O'Brien, and suspicion of the sexual assault against a minor. You are now under arrest. I am now going to inform you of your rights. You have the right to remain silent, anything you say and do can be used against you in a court of law. You have the right to attain legal counsel during questioning. If you cannot afford legal counsel the court will appoint someone to you. You also have the right to end questioning at any time. Do you understand you rights as I read them to you?"

The Politician had turned bright red, "Don't be so foolish. You imbecile, you can't arrest me!" He started to struggle. The officers got either side of him, lifted him a little and went off with him like some unruly naughty child being chastised by his parents. Some people attending the surgery cheered and clapped loudly. The officers bundled him into the back of the police car and drove to Leeds central police station.

Exquisite Beauty

The Artist stared at Tess. She was exquisite. As perfect as ever. He spoke to her, "Not long now darling girl. Can't believe I lost you the first time. Do you like the ceiling? It's very Sedlec Ossuary isn't it? It's very you, Tess. My family have been creating this for centuries. It has taken a lot of bones dear girl to create such beauty."

Tess stuck out her chin, like she did as a teenager, challenging him.

"No, because the Sedlec Ossuary is a sacred place, the soil in which they were buried was from the Holy Land itself. The Artist, well woodcarver, was much more talented than you will ever be. The ceiling will look better though once you are dead and your hung up alongside them," she spat at him. She wasn't going to die like a scared little girl, for she no longer was. He was puny and pathetic, not the big monster in her dreams.

He tilted his head to one side, "How ungrateful of you, Tess. I merely wanted to offer you to the gods in an archaeological fashion. Don't you see the beauty of being buried with the swan wings and grave goods? I thought you were an academic for God's sake."

He was angry now but not nearly as angry as Tess. Hee had practically stolen her life for all those years and other things she could never retrieve. She had loosened the rope that bound her hands behind her back. The stupid man hadn't even checked her person. She had mistakenly put sharp callipers in her back pocket, ones she used to help measure distances of teeth and other parts of skeletal remains. In fact when she was talking to Dylan they were pricking her backside.

She moved stealthy grabbing the callipers and launched herself at the Artist. He was startled and knocked off balance. They grappled on the floor but she still held onto them. He started to choke her. She looked him straight in the eyes and stabbed him in his jugular vein. Blood spurted everywhere, drenching her like a scene in a horror movie. This was a horror movie, the end of the horror movie.

Closing In

Mike had followed Dina, Andy and Mimmy into the castle, it was like a cathedral. They entered a large entrance hall with numerous doors leading off to different rooms and other halls. The tiles under foot were black and white diamond shapes and it reminded Mike of the Mad Hatter's tea party. Dina took a deep breath willing herself on. This castle held many memories mainly horrific ones for her. Police officers were also searching and shouting for Tess. They looked in many rooms; the laundry, servants quarters, the great dining room, the kitchen, four living rooms all with grand fireplaces, Chesterfield sofas, overstuffed chairs in some rooms, other rooms far grander with detailed embroidered couches and chaise lounges. The found nothing. They headed upstairs on the sweeping staircase passing expensive portraits of ancestors up to the different wings and bedrooms, all ten of them. Fancy four poster beds and French furniture dressed most rooms. Drapes over windows were embossed with pictures of elegant women and gents from long gone eras. They opened wardrobes, cupboards and looked under beds. Still nothing. They went down into the bowels of the building. It felt like descending to hades. None of the grand regalia here just very tight winding stone stairs, bare stone walls and the dinginess gave an eerier feel.

Tess pushed a very dead Artist off of her. She rolled over and gagged at the thought of his body touching hers. She glanced down at his blood-soaked body just to make sure he was gone, and he was. She raised her foot back and booted him in his side, for no other reason that it felt good and he had it coming. She looked around for an escape route but couldn't see any. There must be a door or some exit she thought. It was like being trapped in some sort of escape room. There seemed lots of trickery in here, like doors had been camouflaged either to make it difficult to exit, fun or both. She heard a noise in the wall behind her and turned in that direction, a panel exploded from its place onto the floor and a very large male jumped down a few metres to the floor.

"Oh, thank God," said Tess. "Help at last," as she dashed towards the man.

The man nodded solemnly and put out his hand motioning for her to shake it. Tess shook his hand vigorously.

"Hey I'm Tess, are you one of Patrick's colleagues?"

She smiled and then tried to back off when she saw the ragged scar on the man's cheek.

"Paul," he nodded in the direction of the very dead Artist.

"He was my boss and friend." He punched Tess in the face before she had a chance to run or protest. He dragged her by her ponytail over to his boss so he could check for vitals. He dropped her like a sack of potatoes and the back of her head hit the stone floor hard. Tess was barely conscious. He knelt down, at the side of the Artist and checked for a pulse, all the while knowing he was dead. He sobbed, then stood up over Tess and started kicking her.

Dylan Interview Room 1

He had gone with the police voluntarily. The police wanted to take him to hospital to get him checked out but he said the police doctor could do that, there was urgency about him. He was now wifeless and childless. His wife had cried, screamed and threw anything she could in his direction calling him a fucking coward, as if he needed reminding. Anyhow he couldn't have a wife in jail, could he? Hopefully he could reconcile when his kids were older.

The police doctor checked him over. Administered pain relief, said he had a few broken ribs which they couldn't do anything about anyway. Then he was led to the interview room, passing a well-dressed man who was under arrest and shouting and screaming at everyone. There was quite a commotion. The interview room was stuffy with the heat of summer. It was painted white, no frills or expense in this room that was for sure. Windowless for obvious reasons, harsh strip lights glared down, making the room only hotter.

He was offered water which he took then sat down in front of 2 detectives. They looked intimidating. They had some sort of recording device and cameras were trained on them at all times recording every single thing. He had been offered representation by a criminal solicitor which he accepted but informed the woman he would be pleading guilty. He didn't want a reduction in his sentence. He just wanted to pay for his involvement in both kidnaps of Teresa O'Brien.

His solicitor was a good looking woman, aged about 40, tall like a supermodel. She introduced herself as Kerris. She spoke with a soft Scottish accent and whispered to him making sure he understood all charges against him. He nodded affirmatively. .

Dylan told his story, from his hideous early childhood with his father, his attraction to a teenage Tess, his involvement in her first kidnap. He let out a gasp and cried on hearing of her rape. Between sobs he carried on with his story, thinking of his own daughters, of his wife, and his mother. He spoke of his absolute fear of his father and the control he held over he and his mother, even long after he had left. He explained that his father had made threats against his mother. If Dylan didn't assist him they would all be mercilessly tormented.

DCI Bridges held out her hand to stop Dylan. Her colleague DCI Redmond paused the recorder. They stared at each other, what Dylan was saying raining down on them like blows to their heads.

DCI Bridges spoke, "So, Dylan, your father Paul was taking Tess to his boss? He was kidnapping her for someone else? The man that calls himself the Artist?"

"Yes, exactly that." Dylan looked confused.

"So your father will be on the scene with his boss and Tess?"

"Yes," Dylan replied while he took a gulp of water.

His solicitor leaned forward, "May I ask what's going on please?"

"Yes," said DCI Redmond, "the police and group that are searching for Tess are in greater danger than we thought. We thought we had one perpetrator?"

He pulled out his mobile phone from his jacket pocket, left the room and called Mike. Answer phone, oh fuck no! He went to reception told the duty sergeant that they must try and contact

Mike and the local Scottish police force attending the search. The sergeant nodded and went to it straight away, sensing the danger.
DCI Redmond went back to the interview room and asked for recording to begin and that Dylan continued.

Dylan reiterated his father's threats to him, the vile child porn his father had put on his computer, he explained he didn't know how this happened just that more recently it seemed like his father had wanted to build bridges. He had been to visit his family and asked to use their computer for something. That's the only thing Dylan could think of. He requested they speak to his mother about his father's previous actions? He gave any information he possessed about his father's car and possibly where he lived. He also requested that they didn't refer to him as that, his father but as Paul. Both DCI'S nodded in agreement. Dylan was returned to his cell

The Politician Interview Room 2

Room 2 was even more drab and claustrophobic than room 1. The same DCIS were about to interview the politician as they were heading the investigation. They poured 3 cups of water, nodded to each other to proceed, DCI Redmond clicked the recording device. The politician sat stony faced with his well-dressed solicitor, his suit pinstriped looked like expensive Saville Row, a deep purple sink handkerchief in the breast pocket, the solicitor introduced himself stony faced.

"Mr Bowden, representing my client Laird Bruferry of Argyll, Now let's get on with this charade, my clients a busy man." He twisted his face in disgust.

DCI Bridges read him his rights. Then asked him to clarify his full name.

The politician whispered something angrily to his solicitor.

"You know very well I am Laird Bruferry of Argyll." He looked at them both like a fly that had landed on his food. "Lord or Laird, for God's sake."

DCI Redmond spoke into the microphone. "The suspect is being uncooperative and difficult." He looked across sternly at the politician.

"Answer," is all his solicitor said.

The politician cleared his throat, "Lord or Laird Cameron-Blair, Bruferry of Argyll. This is absurd," he bellowed.

DCI Bridges glared at him, daring him to raise his voice again and then began questioning him.

"In April 2000 did you sexually assault a child at her school premises in Leeds?"

The politician sat stony faced then answered, "What? How on earth would I even recollect where I was so long ago? And no I did not," raising his voice again. His solicitor made a shushing gesture with his hand, non-verbally requesting he didn't raise his voice.

"In 2007 did you have any knowledge about the kidnap and whereabouts of Teresa O'Brien?"

"WHO? WHO is that?" he glared at the DCIS

"Have you any information about the recent abduction of Teresa O'Brien, DR O'Brien?" DCI Bridges was losing patience.

"No Comment," He smirked.

"Do you have any information regarding the kidnap of a Ms Gina Donovan?"

"No Comment," he dragged his words purposely.

DCI Redmond took over. He shoved a sealed plastic evidence bag towards the Politician and his solicitor, "Do you recognise this item, exhibit 1?" It was the detectives turn to smirk.

"No Comment," but something in his voice was not as confident.

"Did you purchase this item from Cartier, London for the price of 12k?" DCI Redmond grinned.

The Politician and his solicitor whispered, his solicitor looking increasingly alarmed.

DCI Bridges took over again, "Lord," she said out loudly over accentuating the word. "Cameron-Blair Bruferry, you are under arrest for the sexual assault of a minor, Ms Teresa O'Brien, the involvement in kidnapping a minor, Ms Teresa O'Brien, two charges of kidnapping one Ms Gina Donovan and Dr Teresa O'Brien, still missing, I strongly advise that you start talking," she turned to her colleague and gave a quick smile.

Then And Now

David had returned to the lab with the police officer, they would be sending the information he and Tess had discovered about the skeleton or skeletons and teeth over to the police then they would run dental checks on missing persons. They had already handed the evidence of the bracelet to DCI Redmond and Bridges. David just hoped they would be in time to save Tess.

A police car met Tess's devastated parents at the airport. They consoled each other in the back of the car as the police officer drove them to the nearest station.

Tess was barely conscious as the blows kept raining down on her, she dreamt though, of two strikingly similar men who had hurt her alongside the man that was hurting her now.

Mimmy stopped Mike, Dina and Andy. "I have just remembered that as a child I had found a secret room deep down in the bowels of the castle, one I'd never encountered before. It was scary, the ceilings decorated with skeletons and a huge chandelier made from skulls hung down. I thought I saw a girl sleeping on a chaise lounge. He caught me, that man, call him what you will but not my father or uncle. I despise him. He said she was just posing for her portrait and if I mentioned it I wouldn't see Dina again so I kept quiet." She beckoned them follow her. They all ran.

Back at the police station now, David told DCI Redmond and Bridges what they had found. The teeth had matched the dental records of a missing girl who had vanished 20 years ago from Dunoon Argyll and Bute. It was 15 year old Isla Carmichael. She had been residing in a home for unruly children when she vanished, as was often no one really cared too much, thought she had absconded back to Dundee. The second was possibly a match. A girl who had old breaks in both tibias due to childhood abuse had come up on the missing persons software. One of the partial skeletons had breaks in both tibias. The third skeletal remains were archaic and confusing. They got to work on clarifying the second skeleton, David watched as both DCI's searched data bases.

The Perfect Dying Swan

Paul stopped beating Tess, instead loomed over her getting off on the sight of blood. He was glad his boss the Artist had never found out what he had done to Tess. That wasn't in the plans. Hey though who could resist. He knew what his boss did to his muse's so would finish his boss's work. He also knew his boss picked the finest specimens just like Picasso picked his. In fact Tess somewhat resembled Sylvette David, Picasso's French/English muse. Their natural beauty and elegance obvious. He looked down, she didn't look particularly elegant now, blood gurgled from her mouth, bruising and swelling round her lips and eyes. Did he want to rape her again? No, she was a little too old for his tastes and the politician's, his boss though, his dead boss the Artist was infatuated with her.

He had the swan's wing that he was retrieving for his boss when she killed him. He placed it on the floor then dragged her body placing it gently on top of the swan's wing. It actually looked like the wing was hers, protruding from her body. He took out his phone and started to take pictures of her. After all he was no artist himself. She opened her eyes and stared at him, then nodded slowly groaning in pain as she did. How the fuck was this bitch still alive he thought. Ok they would play hard ball. He straddled her and smiled. He put both hands round her throat and choked her. It would be a noisy death. All he could hear was coughing and spluttering. He didn't hear the blow coming from behind him.

Mimmy had led them to a door like in giant rabbit warren. She pointed to a door that was ajar. Mike put his finger to his lips to silence them, then held up his hand palm out telling them to stay. Mike crept inside the room hearing a gurgling sound as he did. He spotted a man over Tess strangling the life out of her. He ran at the man punching him in the temple knocking him out. Mike cuffed the man's hands behind his back straight away. He shouted to the others who came rushing in. Mimmy crouched down to Tess checking her vitals. She put Tess in the recovery position just in case. She was concerned that Tess would vomit or choke on blood. Mike had no signal down here so Dina ran back upstairs alerting any officers she could. The ambulance service was called straight away.

The Dead Swan

DCI's Redmond, Bridges and David matched the victim. The poor girl was just 20 years old, Sarah Emelia James. She had been the victim of horrific child abuse, social services missing it constantly. Finally, when she had been rescued by authorities aged just 3 she had been admitted to hospital where they found old breaks to the poor child's Tibia. Taken into care she had fared well, not really academic but she had been a talented dancer. She had eventually applied for university and was accepted. The university and her friends had reported her missing, she had no family that cared enough not in the beginning or the end of her life. The end of her life cruel, cut short and for what? Plus the foetuses, their lives snuffed out too. David then received a call from Mike, they had found Tess she was on her way to hospital, protesting all the way. He had found artwork that would maybe put a face to their main victim, he told David about that room with the bones and skull decorations, David nodded knowingly.

The Living Swan

Tess had been rushed to hospital. In the end an air ambulance had taken her, no one wanted to risk her life or wellbeing. Her parents met her there, holding her hands, crying and soothing her. She asked for Patrick, they all looked at Mike for answers, he didn't know anything yet, he tried not to let Tess see his tears. Mike watched as Tess was led away by doctors and nurses to be checked over. His phone rang, it was Gina.

'Gina, please tell me he's alive?'

The End

Acknowledgements

I would like to thank all my family and friends they know who they are, and special thanks to my husband Steven Patrick Docherty for his encouragement belief and support.

Lindsay
August
2024

Author

Lindsay Marie Docherty

I grew up in a working class background. Born in Yorkshire to my mum Lorna and Glaswegian dad Tommy, along with siblings Iain and Kirsty. I worked in casinos until I was 40. I studied law undergraduate and then much later archaeological research with the University of the Highlands and Islands. My love of archaeology led me to the creation of Tess O'Brien. I love to write and although enjoyed writing academically. I prefer the freedom of creating fiction with no constraints. Currently I work in support work working with complex needs.

Publisher

Inherit The Earth

inherit_theearth@btinternet.com

Notes

Amazon KDP

Printed in Great Britain
by Amazon